GO Bible™

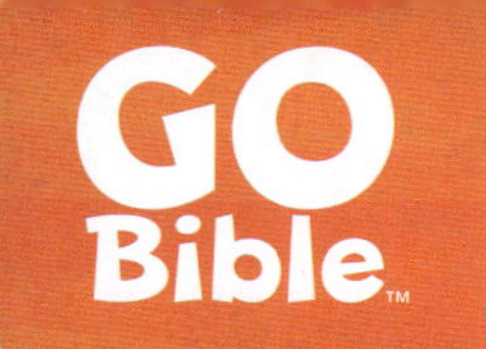

Key Verse CHALLENGE

Scripture Memory Verse Cards

TYNDALE KIDS

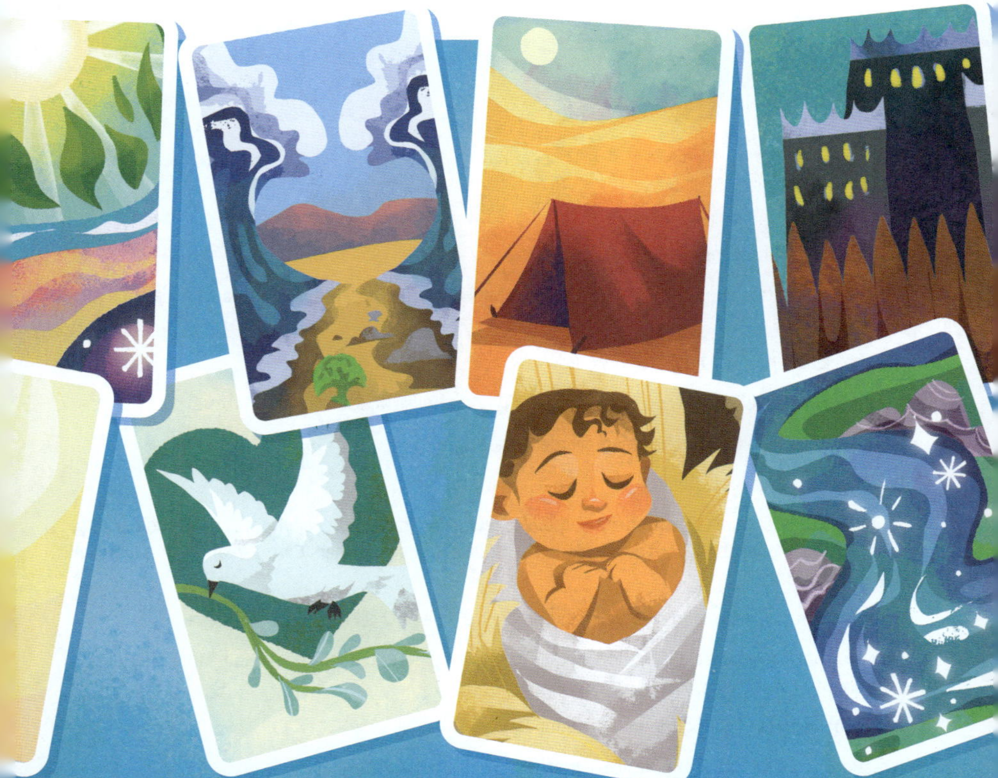

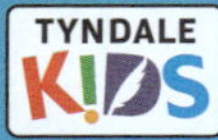

Tyndale House Publishers
Carol Stream, Illinois

Brock Eastman
with Talia Messina

Visit Tyndale's website for kids at tyndale.com/kids.

Tyndale is a registered trademark of Tyndale House Ministries. The Tyndale Kids logo is a trademark of Tyndale House Ministries.

Key Verse Challenge: Scripture Memory Cards

Key Verse Challenge features copyright © 2024 by Tyndale House Ministries. All rights reserved.

Illustrations copyright © Sarah Demonteverde. All rights reserved.

Designed by Jacqueline L. Nuñez

Scripture quotations are taken from the *Holy Bible*, New Living Translation, copyright © 1996, 2004, 2015 by Tyndale House Foundation. Used by permission of Tyndale House Publishers, Carol Stream, Illinois 60188. All rights reserved.

For manufacturing information regarding this product, please call 1-855-277-9400.

For information about special discounts for bulk purchases, please contact Tyndale House Publishers at csresponse@tyndale.com, or call 1-855-277-9400.

Library of Congress Cataloging-in-Publication Data

A catalog record for this book is available from the Library of Congress.

ISBN 979-8-4005-0025-1

Printed in China

30	29	28	27	26	25	24
7	6	5	4	3	2	1

Contents

Introduction

Memorization might sound boring, but did you know that you're memorizing things all the time? How long does it take you to memorize the lyrics to a new song? Or the jersey numbers of your favorite players? How about the fastest bike route to the ice cream shop?

Remembering words, numbers, or places is not hard when it's fun. That's why this Scripture memory guide is bursting with over one hundred fun ways to memorize Bible verses.

Key Verse Challenge Cards

What's so special about remembering verses from the Bible? Bible verses carry wisdom from God to help you when you are confused, worried, lonely, or scared. They bring encouragement when you most need it, but more importantly, they remind you of what is true.

Even Jesus used Bible verses when he was tempted by the devil (see Matthew 4:1-11). After Jesus was baptized, he went into the wilderness alone for forty days. During that time, Satan lied to him a lot. And Satan didn't tell wild lies that sounded fake. Satan twisted the truth of God's words into lies when he tried to tempt Jesus to worship him. Jesus could not be fooled. He had been studying the Scriptures since he was a boy. He caught the lies, and he protected himself from Satan by declaring the true words of God.

You can be like Jesus by memorizing the verses in this book! This Scripture memory guide is packed with some of the most powerful verses in the Bible. Plus, each tear-out card has an activity on the back to help you remember it.

You'll enjoy a wide range of ways to memorize, including

- drawing a picture
- creating crafts that will remind you of the verse
- inventing a song with hand motions
- bouncing a ball for each word of the verse

Some of the activities will encourage you to ask your parents or guardians for stories. For example, the activity for Isaiah 40:31 encourages you to ask an adult about a hard time in their life where God showed up. These are great ways to help you understand the verse better and see how its truth applies to your life.

The best part about these cards is that you can take them wherever you go because they are meant to be torn out.

Encouragement Cards

The encouragement cards are tear-outs you can share with others or keep for yourself.

If you keep them . . .

- Tape them on your bathroom mirror to read while you brush your teeth.
- Slide them into your homework planner for daily reminders of God's love.
- Hole-punch the top left corner of each card and bind them all together with a ring clip. Hook it to your backpack to have the cards with you always.

If you share them . . .

- Slide one into a friend's desk or lunch box if they're having a bad day or they're nervous about a test, game, or performance. They'll appreciate your thoughtfulness!
- Put them inside birthday cards, thank-you cards, or holiday cards.
- Place one by the bathroom sink at school for a classmate to find.
- Leave one in a Little Free Library box or on a neighbor's windshield.
- Mail one to a friend. Even if they live close by, it's always fun to get mail!

You and your friends will grow closer to God as you learn more about his amazing promises!

What's on My Card?

FRONT

Bible book art from *Go Bible*

This is how God loved the world: He gave his one and only Son, so that everyone who believes in him will not perish but have eternal life.

John 3:16

Verse

Book Chapter Verse number

BACK

Activity

Find a friend or family member and make up actions together to go with this verse. Say the verse out loud as you do the actions. Keep practicing until you have memorized this truth about God sending his Son for us—no peeking!

Everything you need to memorize a Bible verse is on these tear-out Key Verse Challenge cards. Each card includes the Bible verse and the verse reference.

Verse references are like house addresses. When you get a letter in the mail, the envelope says your name, house number, street name, town, state, and zip code. Bible verse references are simpler. They tell you the book, chapter, and verse number. If you want to know more about the verse you are memorizing or understand how it fits in the Bible story, look it up using the Bible reference.

Find the Verse Reference

Let's say you want to look up John 3:16.

1. Go to the table of contents near the front of your Bible and find the book named John. This is kind of like your town name in your address. (Psst! This one is a little tricky because there are four books with the name John in them: John, 1 John, 2 John, and 3 John. But they are all different! For this example, just look for John.)

3

2. Once you're in the book of John, turn the pages until you get to a big number 3. This is the chapter number. It's like your street name.

3. Within chapter 3, look for a smaller number 16. This is the verse number. It's like your house number.

Key Verse Challenge
JOHN 3:16
Find a friend or family member and make up actions together to go with this verse. Say the verse out loud as you do the actions. Keep practicing until you have memorized this truth about God sending his Son for us—no peeking!

Jesus and Nicodemus

23Because of the miraculous signs Jesus did in Jerusalem at the Passover celebration, many began to trust in him. 24But Jesus didn't trust them, because he knew all about people. 25No one needed to tell him about human nature, for he knew what was in each person's heart.

3 There was a man named Nicodemus, a Jewish religious leader who was a Pharisee. 2After dark one evening, he came to speak with Jesus. "Rabbi," he said, "we all know that God has sent you to teach us. Your miraculous signs are evidence that God is with you."

3Jesus replied, "I tell you the truth, unless you are born again, you cannot see the Kingdom of God."

"What do you mean?" exclaimed Nicodemus. "How can an old man go back into his mother's womb and be born again?"

5Jesus replied, "I assure you, no one can enter the Kingdom of God without being born of water and the Spirit. 6Humans can reproduce only human life, but the Holy Spirit gives birth to spiritual life. 7So don't be surprised when I say, 'You must be born again.' 8The wind blows wherever it wants. Just as you can hear the wind but can't tell where it comes from or where it is going, so you can't explain how people are born of the Spirit."

9"How are these things possible?" Nicodemus asked.

10Jesus replied, "You are a respected Jewish teacher, and yet you don't understand these things? 11I assure you, we tell you what we know and have seen, and yet you won't believe our testimony. 12But if you don't believe me when I tell you about earthly things, how can you possibly believe if I tell you about heavenly things? 13No one has ever gone to heaven and returned. But the Son of Man has come down from heaven. 14And as Moses lifted up the bronze snake on a pole in the wilderness, so the Son of Man must be lifted up, 15so that everyone who believes in him will have eternal life.

16"For this is how God loved the world: He gave his one and only Son, so that everyone who believes in him will not perish but have eternal life. 17God sent his Son into the world not to judge the world, but to save the world through him.

18"There is no judgment against anyone who believes in him. But anyone who does not believe in him has already been judged for not believing in God's one and only Son. 19And the judgment is based on this fact: God's light came into the world, but people loved the darkness more than the light, for their actions were evil. 20All who do evil hate the light and refuse to go near it for fear their sins will be exposed. 21But those who do what is right come to the light so others can see that they are doing what God wants."

John the Baptist Exalts Jesus

22Then Jesus and his disciples left Jerusalem and went into the Judean countryside. Jesus spent some time with them there, baptizing people.

23At this time John the Baptist was baptizing at Aenon, near Salim, because there was plenty of water there; and people kept coming to him for baptism. 24(This was before John was thrown into prison.) 25A debate broke out between John's disciples and a certain Jew over ceremonial cleansing. 26So John's disciples came to him and said, "Rabbi, the man you met on the other side of the

Match the Art

Have you noticed the bright and colorful artwork on your cards? Some cards have the same artwork. Can you guess why? Line them up together and see if you can spot something similar.

Did you notice that cards with the same artwork all come from the same book of the Bible? If you want to memorize verses from the same book at the same time, you can match them up by their art.

The Books of the Bible

Old Testament

Genesis
Exodus
Leviticus
Numbers
Deuteronomy
Joshua
Judges
Ruth
1 Samuel
2 Samuel
1 Kings
2 Kings
1 Chronicles
2 Chronicles
Ezra
Nehemiah
Esther
Job
Psalms
Proverbs
Ecclesiastes
Song of Songs
Isaiah
Jeremiah

Lamentations
Ezekiel
Daniel
Hosea
Joel
Amos
Obadiah
Jonah
Micah
Nahum
Habakkuk
Zephaniah
Haggai
Zechariah
Malachi

New Testament

Matthew
Mark
Luke
John
Acts
Romans
1 Corinthians

2 Corinthians
Galatians
Ephesians
Philippians
Colossians
1 Thessalonians
2 Thessalonians
1 Timothy
2 Timothy
Titus

Philemon
Hebrews
James
1 Peter
2 Peter
1 John
2 John
3 John
Jude
Revelation

The Books of the Bible in Alphabetical Order

Acts	Joel
Amos	John
1 Chronicles	1 John
2 Chronicles	2 John
Colossians	3 John
1 Corinthians	Jonah
2 Corinthians	Joshua
Daniel	Jude
Deuteronomy	Judges
Ecclesiastes	1 Kings
Ephesians	2 Kings
Esther	Lamentations
Exodus	Leviticus
Ezekiel	Luke
Ezra	Malachi
Galatians	Mark
Genesis	Matthew
Habakkuk	Micah
Haggai	Nahum
Hebrews	Nehemiah
Hosea	Numbers
Isaiah	Obadiah
James	1 Peter
Jeremiah	2 Peter
Job	Philemon

Philippians

Proverbs

Psalms

Revelation

Romans

Ruth

1 Samuel

2 Samuel

Song of Songs

1 Thessalonians

2 Thessalonians

1 Timothy

2 Timothy

Titus

Zechariah

Zephaniah

Introduction to the New Living Translation

When we want to read something that's written in another language, it needs to be translated into our own language. *Translate* means to put the words and meanings of one language into the words of another language. The Bible was first written in languages that most people today don't know, so it has been translated into many modern languages, including English.

The Bible translation you hold in your hands was designed to be easy for you to read and understand. We hope that you will meet the living God when you read it. And we hope that you will be changed by encountering him. This introduction answers a few questions you might have about Bible translation and the New Living Translation (which we call the NLT).

Where did the Bible come from?

The Bible is the grand story of God, people, and the world we live in. It is God's Word for us. God didn't write down the Bible himself. Through his Spirit—the Holy Spirit—he spoke to people. Those people wrote down his words and actions for all of us to read. There are sixty-six sections in the Bible, and we call these sections "books."

Many Bible books began as stories that were passed down through many generations. Then people wrote these stories down and collected them so they could be shared with everyone. Some Bible books were speeches or poems that people wrote down. Other books tell the history of God's people. Others are letters that were written to churches or individuals to answer their questions or teach them about God.

God's people continued to read and share these books over many years. Then the books were gathered into two groups. The Old Testament has thirty-nine books. These books tell the story of how God chose the Israelites to be his people and point the world to God.

The New Testament has twenty-seven books. These books include the stories of Jesus and his earliest followers. They also include letters that some of these followers sent to churches. As a whole, the Bible gives us God's unique message for all people.

Why do we translate the Bible?

We translate the Bible so we can read it in the language we speak. The Old Testament was first written mostly in Hebrew. The New Testament was first written in Greek. Now, through translation, we can read the Bible in our own language.

The NLT translators wanted to help readers understand the message of the Bible. They accurately translated the words of the original languages into clear English. And they were extra careful to use words and phrases that make sense to today's readers.

How was the NLT created?

A Bible translation team was formed that included Bible experts and English-language experts. Small teams of the Bible experts worked together to translate each book of the Bible into English. Then the English-language experts worked hard to make sure the translation was easy to understand. After that, the Bible Translation Committee, which included some of the Bible experts and English-language experts, reviewed the translation. Each Bible book went through many reviews and revisions by these teams. After that, the Bible Translation Committee agreed on the final translation.

What kinds of decisions did the translators make?

All languages change over time, so some of the words in older English Bible translations can be confusing to us. To create an easy-to-read translation, the NLT translators used words and phrases common to most English speakers today.

The translators made choices to help modern readers understand the Bible. They translated the words in the Bible for units of weight, measurement, and money into modern American terms, like pounds, inches, and numbers of coins. They also translated dates to match our modern calendar.

The original languages and cultures of the Bible used words like "man" or "brothers" when they meant both women and men. In today's English, we usually use words that include everyone when we refer to groups of people. An important example of this is found in the New Testament letters. Christians were often called "brothers" in Greek. But the writers had both men and women in mind. So the NLT translates this Greek word as "brothers and sisters" to represent the meaning of the original texts.

How does the Bible sound?

We learn from the Bible itself that these books are meant to be read aloud in community and public worship (see Nehemiah 8:2-3; 1 Timothy 4:13; Revelation 1:3). We still read the Bible out loud in families, small groups, and church. Because of this, the translators wanted the NLT to be clear and understandable when read out loud. They wanted the hearers of the NLT to have a deep and exciting experience with the Bible.

●　●　●

Translating the Bible is a big and important task that is never finished. The translators prayed for God's guidance and wisdom while they worked to translate the NLT. We hope this translation will bless and help the church and all people—including you.

The Publishers

Transformation Themes

No matter which book of the Bible we turn to, we read about God transforming people's lives . . . and transforming the world! This list gives a preview of God's work of transformation in each book.

Genesis: Here at the beginning, we start to learn about God's plan of transformation for his people and his world. Though sin hurt God's creation, it couldn't stop his purpose to make things right again.

Exodus: God transformed the lives of his people by setting them free from slavery in Egypt, showing them how to obey him, and keeping all his promises to them.

Leviticus: God is holy and perfect. When God chose the Israelites to be his people, he transformed them into a holy people. God gave the Israelites his law so they could live in God's holy presence and worship him rightly.

Numbers: The Israelites complained and doubted God on their way to the Promised Land. But during their time wandering, God transformed them so they would be ready to live in the land when they returned later.

Deuteronomy: God gives his people the choice between turning away from him and obeying him. Obeying and serving God may not always be easy, but it results in an amazingly transformed life.

Joshua: The Israelites went from wandering in the desert to settling down in the land God gave them. Through Joshua's leadership, we see God keeping his promises to his people.

Judges: Even though the Israelites kept falling into the same sin patterns, God showed them mercy over and over again—and he does the same for us.

Ruth: God has the power to transform even the most hopeless circumstances.

1 Samuel: Human kings weren't able to transform the hearts of the people—but God is able, and he never lets his people down.

2 Samuel: When we turn back to God after we sin, he is always ready to forgive, but we may still face the consequences in our lives.

1 Kings: When we follow God and listen to wise advice, we'll get to know God better and become more like him. The opposite is also true: when we disobey God, it gets easier to keep turning away from him.

2 Kings: Even when there's disobedience all around, God can help us choose a different path—and he can give us the strength to stick to it when it's hard.

1 Chronicles: This book was written to remind God's people of the way he transformed Israel into a nation. God was faithful in the past, and he will be faithful in the future.

2 Chronicles: God disciplines those he loves because he wants their lives to change from rebellion to obedience.

Ezra: God worked in the hearts of idol-worshiping kings so they allowed the Israelites to rebuild the Temple. Even more than transforming the Temple, God wants to transform his people's hearts.

Nehemiah: God cares about his people and keeps his promises to them. He gave the people everything they needed to rebuild the wall of Jerusalem in less than two months.

Esther: God can take us from doubt and fear to courageous confidence—and give us a key role in his work.

Job: Job didn't understand why he was suffering, but he didn't stop trusting in God's love and power. Seeking God when we're going through hard times can transform us into people of greater faith too.

Psalms: This book of poetry is filled with prayers of pain as well as songs of thankfulness and praise. When we are honest with God about our pain, he can bring peace and hope to our hearts. And when we worship God, we will experience great joy!

Proverbs: This book shows the importance of living wisely and respecting God. We can ask God to help us grow wiser as we get to know him more and more.

Ecclesiastes: It's easy to want things like money and popularity. But what matters most in life isn't earthly stuff—it's following, loving, and obeying God. We can ask God to transform our hearts so we learn to care about what really matters.

Song of Songs: In our world, we often see a shallow, fickle kind of love. This book shows how God wants to transform our view of love and marriage and give us his wisdom about this part of life.

Isaiah: The prophet Isaiah warned the people of his day to turn away from their sin and back to God. He also describes what the world will be like when God makes everything new.

Jeremiah: Despite being mocked, beaten, and put in prison, Jeremiah kept urging the people of Judah to ask God for forgiveness. He also prophesied about the heart transformation that Jesus would bring.

Lamentations: The people of Judah were exiled to Babylon and Jerusalem was destroyed because of their disobedience. But God did not abandon them—he had a good plan for them, and he would bring them back to their home.

Ezekiel: God promised to transform his sinful people when they asked for forgiveness—and to restore their relationship with him. Guess what? He does the same thing today!

Daniel: When we stand firm in our faith, God can work through us in big ways to transform the lives of those around us.

Hosea: The people of Israel had turned away from God. They received consequences for their sins, but God promised to bring them back to him because of his great love for them.

Joel: God's people struggled to follow him, but Joel saw a future where God's people return to him and the Holy Spirit transforms their lives.

Amos: Amos's message was for people who cared more about storing up riches than about helping others in need. God called them to leave their selfish sin and live generously instead, and he calls us to do the same.

 **Obadiah:** God wants his people to move from pride and self-centeredness toward kindness and humility.

Jonah: The people of Nineveh did terrible things, but when Jonah finally shared God's message with them, they listened. God forgave the people of Nineveh because they turned to him.

Micah: God's people had turned their backs on him, and judgment was coming. But God is the master of bringing life from death. Micah shared about God's transforming power and how he would give his people a new start.

Nahum: God cares about his people, and he won't let their enemies get away with evil forever.

Habakkuk: God can handle our questions, and it's okay to be honest with him about our doubts and fears.

 **Zephaniah:** God told Zephaniah to share some tough news with the people of Judah: their sins would have big consequences. But the story doesn't end there. God would save his people from their suffering and bring them home.

 **Haggai:** God helps his people choose to work hard for him instead of focusing on themselves.

Zechariah: Zechariah had many visions that show God's faithfulness to his people. God keeps his promises, including his promise to send Jesus, who would change the entire world one day.

Malachi: God's people thought he had forgotten about them, but God never leaves his people. God works in his own perfect timing, and when we have doubts or questions, we can turn toward him.

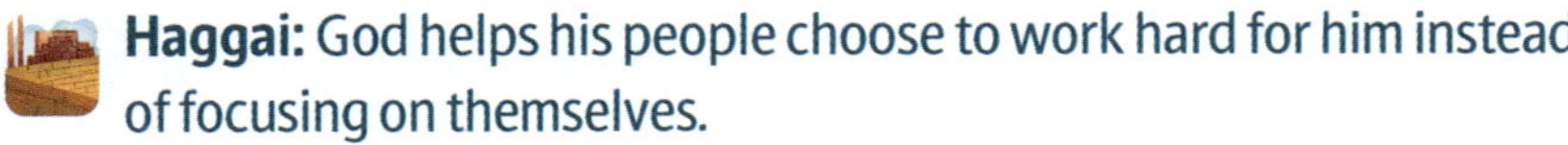

Matthew: Jesus is the only one who can set us free from sin, and he invites us to share this message with everyone. Matthew, the writer of this book, experienced his own transformation from a hated tax collector to a beloved follower of Jesus.

Mark: Jesus transformed the lives of many people through his teaching and miracles. Jesus is alive today, and he continues to change lives around the world.

Luke: Jesus welcomes everyone who has faith in him, no matter where they're from or what they've done.

John: Because of his great love for the world, God sent Jesus to earth. God's good plan has always been to transform lives through the sacrifice of his Son.

Acts of the Apostles: Jesus' life, death, and resurrection had an incredible impact on his friends and followers, so they began telling others about him. We see the Holy Spirit is at work, transforming the lives of all kinds of people.

Romans: We all sin and deserve the punishment of being far from God. But Jesus, who lived a perfect life, chose to die on the cross to take our punishment. Now whoever believes in Jesus and chooses to follow him will be close to God forever!

1 Corinthians: If Jesus has transformed us, we should follow and obey him—not just live like everyone else.

2 Corinthians: The closer we get to Jesus, the more we become like him. Becoming more like Jesus often goes hand in hand with suffering, but Paul didn't let that get in the way of sharing the message of Jesus.

Galatians: Many people teach and believe that we're saved by the good things we do. But we can only be saved by faith in Jesus. When we follow Jesus, we begin to see evidence of transformation in our lives—also known as the fruit of the Spirit.

Ephesians: We are forgiven and transformed the moment we trust Jesus. But the story doesn't end there. We will grow closer to God and become more like him as we choose to follow him each day.

Philippians: Life is not always easy here on earth. But even in hard times, Jesus can give us lasting joy.

Colossians: Jesus is fully man and fully God. He has done everything needed to save us, give us new life, and change our hearts.

1 Thessalonians: God will give us hope when we are treated badly because of our faith. He will also help us look forward to the day when Jesus will come back.

2 Thessalonians: With God's help, we can learn to be wise and tell the difference between lies and the truth of God's Word.

1 Timothy: If we love and believe in Jesus, we are called to live for him, no matter how old we are. We show others what Jesus is like when we follow him.

2 Timothy: The Bible corrects us when we're wrong and leads us to do what's right. God's Word helps us live for Jesus and tell others about him, even when we're afraid.

Titus: As members of God's family, it's important to obey him—but we don't have to do it alone! God will give us the strength we need to trust and follow him.

 **Philemon:** Following Jesus means we must learn to value and care for other people the way Jesus does.

 **Hebrews:** Jesus is worthy of our worship and loyalty, and staying true to him transforms us into people who are faithful followers of Jesus and living in a way that honors him.

James: True faith in Jesus will lead to love for others and obedience to God.

1 Peter: When we decide to follow Jesus, we join God's family. That doesn't mean life will be easy, but it does mean that we'll know he's always with us, helping us through every hard thing.

2 Peter: God will keep all his promises, and he can help us trust him even when we're surrounded by lies.

 **1 John:** When we follow Jesus and know what the Bible says, we can distinguish the darkness of false teaching from the light of God's Word.

 **2 John:** Following Jesus means being set free by the truth and becoming more like him in the way we love others.

 **3 John:** Prayer and God's Word are transformational tools to help us obey John's instruction in this book to "follow only what is good" (3 John 1:11).

Jude: False teachers say followers of Jesus don't have to change their lives. But a transformed life is evidence of a heart transformed by Jesus.

Revelation: One day, Jesus will return to earth and get rid of everything scary or sad. He will make everything right, and followers of Jesus will live forever with him!

Where to Turn When Life Is Hard

The Bible is full of encouraging words and helpful insights. It offers practical advice and is packed with promises from God that we can hold on to in tough times.

Here's a list of powerful passages to turn to when you face difficult times.

When...	Remember...
I'm lonely.	God is always with you (see Isaiah 41:10).
I'm scared.	Don't be afraid. God is with you (see Deuteronomy 31:6).
I'm angry.	Don't let anger control you (see Ephesians 4:26-27).
I don't want to listen to my parents.	Ask God to help you lovingly obey them (see Ephesians 6:1).
I've done something bad.	Confess your sin to God and trust in his forgiveness (see 1 John 1:8-9).
I wonder if heaven is real.	Remember that Jesus is preparing a special place for everyone who believes in him (see John 14:1-3).
My friend is sad.	Encourage them (see 1 Thessalonians 5:11).
My friend is mad at me.	Apologize and do your best to make peace (see Romans 12:18).
Someone was unkind to me.	Forgive them (see Colossians 3:13) and pray for them (see Matthew 5:43-44).
I want to get back at someone.	Be kind to them instead, even when it's hard (see 1 Peter 3:9).
Life doesn't seem fair.	God will bring good things out of bad ones for those who love him (see Romans 8:28).

The World versus the Word

As the messages of the world grow louder and louder, they seem to get further and further away from the truths of God's Word. Sometimes it seems like it would be a whole lot easier to give in and do what the world says is best. But just as Jesus did in the wilderness (Matthew 4:1-11), we can use truths from the Word of God to fight the temptation to believe the world's messages.

The World Says . . .

God's rules are out of date.

Do what feels right.

Trust in yourself.

Focus on what you need.

Hate your enemies.

Hurt those who hurt you.

There's only your truth.

Follow your heart.

Treat others however you want.

Get more for yourself.

God's Word Says . . .

God's rules last forever (see Psalm 119:89).

Do what is right (see Proverbs 21:2-3).

Trust in God (see Proverbs 3:5-6).

Focus on helping others (see Matthew 5:40-42).

Love your enemies (see Matthew 5:44).

Pray for those who hurt you (see Matthew 5:44).

There's only God's truth (see Matthew 7:15; John 14:6).

Follow Jesus (see Matthew 16:24-26).

Treat others how you want to be treated (see Luke 6:31).

Be grateful and generous (see 2 Corinthians 9:6-8).

This is just the beginning. The more you read God's Word, the more truths you'll discover. Make your own list and keep it where you can find it when you need reminders of what God says.

Guide to Following Jesus

Read the Bible

The Bible is God's Word. It's filled with amazing stories, wise words, teachings from Jesus, and more. The Bible is the ultimate source of truth, and it can guide you each and every day.

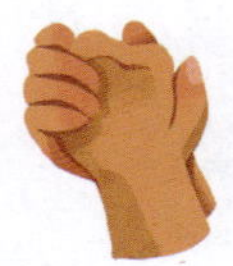

Pray

Prayer is simply talking to God. You can pray anytime, anywhere, and about anything. When you pray, you can praise God, ask him for help, confess your sins and ask forgiveness, and thank God for everything he's done for you.

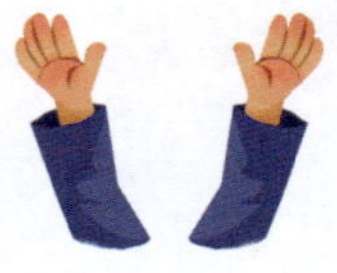

Worship

You can worship God in all sorts of ways. Here are some to try: sing songs of praise, go outside and thank God for his creation, or read the Bible and think deeply about God and his Word.

Connect

Spend time with other people who follow Jesus! You can ask each other questions, read the Bible together, pray as a group, and have fun with each other. If you don't have any Jesus-following friends, ask God to bring them into your life.

Serve

Jesus gave many examples of what it looks like to serve others. Did you know helping people can actually change you, too? As you help others, you'll become more like Jesus, and you'll learn to love them the way he does.

Have you ever wondered why the Bible is so important? Have you had thoughts like *How could a book written thousands of years ago change my life today?* or *Why did God give us the Bible, anyway?* You're not the first person to ask these questions. Let's look at three reasons why the Bible matters.

1. **The Bible is inspired by God.** The Bible is made up of true stories, poems, letters, and more. But they all have one thing in common: they're God's Word. Human authors wrote down the books of the Bible long ago, but God gave them the words to say. We can trust everything the Bible says and get to know God through what he tells us in his Word.

2. **The Bible points us toward Jesus.** Jesus says it himself: "The Scriptures point to me!" (John 5:39). This means the Old Testament promised God's people that Jesus would come to save and lead them. The New Testament shows us how Jesus lived, what he taught, and how his death on the cross made a way for us to be forgiven and transformed. The Bible teaches us everything we need to know about Jesus—and how to receive eternal life from him. It also shows us how to share that great news with other people.

3. **The Bible shows us how to live.** In 2 Timothy 3:16, Paul says Scripture is "useful to teach us what is true and to make us realize what is wrong in our lives. It corrects us when we are wrong and teaches us to do what is right." The more you read the Bible, the more God will teach you how to follow him with your whole life. God's Word changes us from the inside out, making us more and more like him.

The word of God is alive and powerful.
Hebrews 4:12

Jesus and the Old Testament

We often think that Jesus made his arrival in the New Testament when he was born as a human baby. But when we look at the Bible closely, we can see Jesus in the Old Testament, too. Many stories and prophecies in the Old Testament point ahead to the coming of Jesus. And in the New Testament, we see how Jesus' coming to earth, dying on the cross, and rising again were part of the incredible plan God has had since the beginning of time.

Creation

In Genesis 1, we read about God creating the whole universe. The book of John tells us that Jesus, "the Word," existed all the way back then, "in the beginning" (John 1:1-2). Everything was created through Jesus, and he gave life and light to all of creation (John 1:3-4).

Sacrifices and Offerings

The books of Numbers and Leviticus describe a detailed process of sacrifices and offerings to cleanse God's people from their sins. These sacrifices had to happen over and over, and they pointed toward the need for a permanent solution for our sin (see Hebrews 10:1-4). Jesus was "a single sacrifice for sins, good for all time" (Hebrews 10:12). Because of Jesus' death, no further sacrifices are necessary to take away our sin.

The Temple and Priests

In Old Testament times, official worship took place in the Tabernacle or the Temple. The high priest made sure everything was done exactly as God's law said it must be. Now, Jesus is the High Priest of all who follow him: he makes a way for us to be in God's presence and cleans our "guilty consciences" (Hebrews 10:21-22).

Jesus' Teachings

When Jesus taught the people, he quoted the Old Testament all the time. For example, he said that the most important commandment is to "love the Lord your God with all your heart, all your soul, all your mind, and all your strength" (Mark 12:29-30). He was giving the same instruction from God that Moses gave the people all the way back in Deuteronomy 6:4-5.

The Prophets

From our point in history, we can see all the ways the Old Testament prophets point ahead to the coming of Jesus. The prophet Isaiah wrote, "The virgin . . . will give birth to a son and will call him Immanuel (which means 'God is with us')" (Isaiah 7:14). Hundreds of years later, Isaiah's words were fulfilled when Jesus, the Savior of the world, was born in Bethlehem (see Luke 2:11).

The Power of Prayer

What is prayer?

Prayer is how we talk to God. You can pray quietly, in your mind, or by saying your prayer aloud. You can praise God through prayer. You can also thank him for the wonderful things he has done. Through prayer, we can ask for things for ourselves and others—and we can trust that God is always in control, even when we don't see an answer.

How should I pray?

When we pray, we can talk to God about anything—our feelings, our needs, our dreams, and the things we want. Try praying with these steps:

1. Tell God you love him and trust him.
2. Thank him for everything he's done.
3. Ask him to forgive you for your sin.
4. Tell him how you or others are in need, and ask him to help.

Is God really listening to my prayers?

Yes, he is! It doesn't matter who you are, how old you are, where you live, or what language you speak—God hears every prayer.

What should I say when I pray?

Don't worry about coming up with the right words to say. God knows what you're thinking, and in an amazing way, when you run out of words to say, the Holy Spirit will pray for you (Romans 8:26-27).

How often should I pray?

As often as you want! Don't give up praying when times are tough—or when things are going well. You can pray before meals and at bedtime, but also throughout the day. God always likes to hear from us, and prayer is a great way to get to know him better.

The Lord's Prayer

In Matthew 6:9-13, Jesus gave his disciples an example of how to pray. This is called the Lord's Prayer, and it's still a great guide to prayer today!

Our Father in heaven, may your name be kept holy.

May your Kingdom come soon.
May your will be done on earth,
as it is in heaven.

Give us today the food we need,

You can pray these words straight from the Bible, or you can apply them to your life like this:

1. Thank God for how holy and amazing he is. Praise him for what he's done for you.
2. Pray that God's justice and peace would come to the world.
3. Ask that everything will happen the way God wants it to happen.
4. Ask for what you need.
5. Ask God to forgive your sins (and to help you forgive others).
6. Ask for help in doing what is right and to be protected from evil.

and forgive us our sins, as we have forgiven those who sin against us.

And don't let us yield to temptation,

but rescue us from the evil one.

Better Together: The Body of Christ

Have you ever seen a foot walking around by itself? Or an eyeball just bouncing along on the ground? That's probably a big no. Do you know why? Because feet and eyes and hands and elbows and ears are only parts of a body.

In 1 Corinthians 12:12-27, the apostle Paul compares the church—God's people as a whole—to a human body. Like a body, the parts all need each other to get around. The eyes help the feet see where to go. The arms open doors for the feet to walk through. The ears and nose help the eyes to get a louder, smellier picture of what they're seeing. The parts all have special functions that work together to help the body be its best.

Just as a foot is not going to get very far by itself, the church is not going to get very far if we each work alone. We are all different. We look different. We speak different languages. We have different talents and abilities and gifts. "We have all been baptized into one body by one Spirit, and we all share the same Spirit" (1 Corinthians 12:13).

So whatever part you play in the body, play it with all your heart (or all your eyeballs or feet)! When you do, you will help the body of Christ to be the healthiest, happiest body it can be.

Share Your Faith

Sharing your faith means telling other people about Jesus and what he's done in your life. Here are a few ways you can share your faith with those around you:

1. Memorize helpful verses from the Bible to share at just the right time.
2. Write a Bible verse about God's love on a sticky note and leave it for someone to find.
3. Pray for people who don't yet follow Jesus.
4. Tell others about something God has helped you with.
5. Invite friends or classmates to fun events at your church.
6. Say a prayer with someone who needs help.
7. Love other people the way God loves you!

What are some other ways you can think of?

How to Lead Others to Jesus

Following Jesus is the best decision you—or anyone—could ever make! So what about the people in your life who haven't chosen to ask Jesus to be their Leader and Savior yet?

You can help others make the decision to follow Jesus too! In fact, Jesus tells all his followers to share about him with other people (see Matthew 28:19-20). He calls us all to tell people what he has done for us—how he loves and forgives us—and what he can do for them also.

Do you have a friend or family member who might want to know more about following Jesus? It can be scary to talk about your faith sometimes, so here are some steps to get you started.

1. **Pray.** Before you do anything else, pray for the person who doesn't know Jesus. God can give you courage to talk with them, and he can also help you know the right time to do so. God loves this person even more than you do!

2. **Share your story.** One great way to begin a conversation about Jesus is to share what he's done for you. Can you think of a time Jesus helped you with something or answered a prayer? What has changed in your life since you started following Jesus? What's your favorite thing about being a Jesus follower? The answers to these questions are good starting points for sharing your faith.

3. **Be a good listener.** A lot of people have questions about Jesus and about becoming a Christian. It's okay if you don't know all the answers! Being a good listener will show the person you care, and you can always ask a Christian adult about the answers later.

4. **Share what it means to follow Jesus.** Tell the other person that Jesus is the only one who can forgive our sins and transform our lives! Romans 10:9 says, "If you openly declare that

Jesus is Lord and believe in your heart that God raised him from the dead, you will be saved." If the person wants to become a follower of Jesus, you can help them tell Jesus that they believe in him and want him to forgive and lead them. Jesus always says yes to that prayer!

5. **Invite them to church or Sunday school, and tell a Christian adult you trust.** It's wonderful when someone starts following Jesus, but they probably still have a lot to learn. That's why it's important for them to spend time with other Christians and start going to church. A Christian adult can help you invite them—and can pray for them with you.

Questions about Jesus

Is Jesus God?

Yes! In John 1:1, John described Jesus as "the Word" and wrote, "The Word was with God, and the Word was God." And in John 10:30, Jesus himself said, "The Father and I are one."

How did Jesus do miracles?

Even though Jesus is fully human, he is also fully God (see Colossians 2:9). God created the universe simply by speaking, and that same power lives inside Jesus. He is able to heal and transform with just a word or a touch of his hand.

Why didn't Jesus save himself from death on the cross?

He could have—and told Peter that he could have asked for "thousands of angels" to save him (Matthew 26:53). Instead, he followed through with the plan God had for him (see Matthew 26:53-54). He knew his death and resurrection were necessary to make a way for humans to know God.

Where is Jesus now?

When Jesus left the earth over 2,000 years ago, we know that he went to heaven to be with God the Father (see Mark 16:19). But just like God the Father, Jesus is everywhere at once. He's always with us, guiding us through his Holy Spirit.

Does Jesus love me?

Yes, he loves you—so much that he gave his life for you!

Glossary of Terms

Some of the memory verses use words that may be new to you. If you get stuck, use the list of definitions below to help you understand.

Children of God: people who believe that Jesus is the Savior, ask him to forgive their sins, and follow what he teaches in the Bible

Clean heart: a word picture that describes what a person is like when their sins have been forgiven by God

Covenant: a binding promise

Crucify: to kill someone by nailing their hands and feet to a cross

Disciple: a follower of Jesus and his teachings from the Bible

Eternal life: when someone keeps existing after death; for followers of Jesus, it will be spent in the new creation with him

Faith: confident trust and belief in God and in his promises even when you can't physically see him

Gentile: a person who isn't Jewish

Glory: honor, praise, and credit

Good News: the amazing message that Jesus died as a sacrifice for sin; also known as the gospel

Grace: a gift someone doesn't deserve; especially God's love for his people

Kingdom of Heaven/Kingdom of God: refers to God's rule and reign as king over all; also refers to the eternal home of God and his people

Meditate: to focus or reflect on

Mercy: showing someone compassion or forgiveness instead of giving them the punishment they deserve

Messiah: the one God chose to save his people; Jesus is the true Messiah

Most High: a way to refer to God, focusing on how great he is

Redeemer: one who sacrifices or gives up something to save another person from harm

Refuge: shelter, safe place

Repent: to stop disobeying God and choose to obey him

Resurrection: the miracle of being brought back to life eternally after death

Righteous living: obeying God according to the wisdom and commands given by the Bible and loving others in every part of life

Sacrifice: something meaningful that is given up for God or someone else

Savior: someone who rescues from danger or punishment; often used to refer to Jesus, who saves people from sin and death

Sin, sinner: disobeying God, a person who disobeys God

Temptation: something that encourages someone to disobey God

Index of Key Verses

New Testament

1 Corinthians 2:12

1 Corinthians 10:13

1 Corinthians 13:13

1 Corinthians 15:51

2 Corinthians 3:17

2 Corinthians 5:17

2 Corinthians 9:15

Galatians 2:20

Galatians 5:22-23

Galatians 6:9

Ephesians 2:8

Ephesians 3:20

Ephesians 4:23-24

Ephesians 6:10

Philippians 1:6

Philippians 2:4

Philippians 4:13

1 Thessalonians 2:4

1 Thessalonians 5:16-18

1 Timothy 4:12

2 Timothy 1:7

2 Timothy 3:16

2 Timothy 4:7

Titus 3:7

Hebrews 11:1

Hebrews 13:8

James 1:5

1 Peter 3:9

1 Peter 5:7

1 John 1:9

1 John 3:16

1 John 4:9

1 John 4:10

1 John 5:21

Revelation 3:20

Revelation 15:3

In the beginning God created the heavens and the earth.

Genesis 1:1

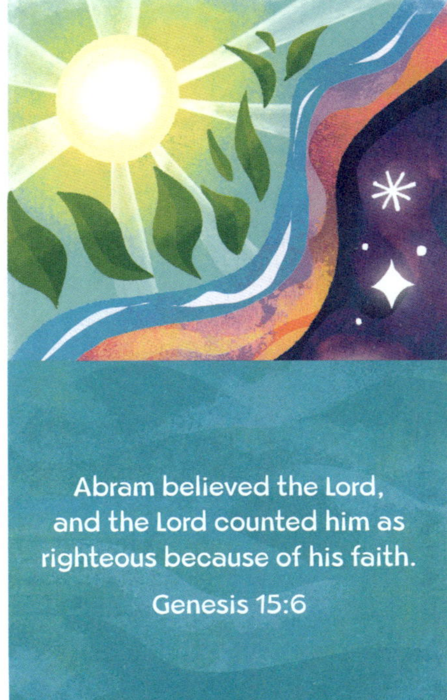

Abram believed the Lord, and the Lord counted him as righteous because of his faith.

Genesis 15:6

You intended to harm me, but God intended it all for good. He brought me to this position so I could save the lives of many people.

Genesis 50:20

Yahweh! The Lord!
The God of compassion and mercy!
I am slow to anger and filled with unfailing love and faithfulness.

Exodus 34:6

Being righteous means doing the right things. Choosing to believe God's promises like Abram did is a righteous thing to do! Read this verse to a friend or family member, and then tell them three promises God makes to us. Look up these additional verses if you need some ideas: Psalm 37:23-24; Matthew 11:28; James 1:5.

Write this verse on a piece of poster board. Then sketch, paint, or doodle images that remind you of God's creation. You could make a nature scene, draw your favorite animal, or sketch a picture of someone you love. Do this on your own, or ask others to help you, and find a place to display it for all to see!

Say this verse out loud, remembering that these are God's own words about himself. Then talk to God and thank him for who he is. You can use this prayer if you want: *Dear God, thank you for being kind and compassionate. You love me no matter what! Help me to be slow to anger like you. Amen.*

Has something happened to you that was no fun but ended up leading to something good? Maybe you really didn't want to change schools, but now you have some awesome friends in your class! Ask an adult to tell you about a time when something hard happened to them and how God used that situation for good. Then read this verse out loud together.

Do not seek revenge or bear a grudge against a fellow Israelite, but love your neighbor as yourself. I am the Lord.

Leviticus 19:18

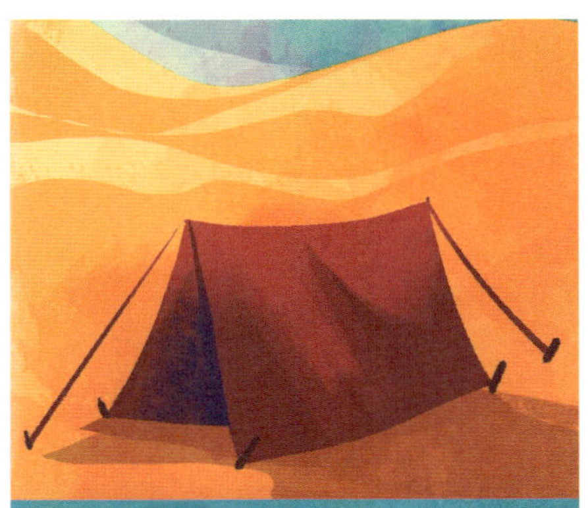

May the Lord bless you and protect you.
May the Lord smile on you and be gracious to you.
May the Lord show you his favor and give you his peace.

Numbers 6:24-26

God is not a man, so he does not lie.
He is not human, so he does not change his mind.
Has he ever spoken and failed to act?
Has he ever promised and not carried it through?

Numbers 23:19

Do not add to or subtract from these commands I am giving you. Just obey the commands of the Lord your God that I am giving you.

Deuteronomy 4:2

Find a dry-erase marker. Think of something that makes you feel scared or anxious, and write it on a whiteboard or a window. Say this verse out loud, remembering that God wants to help you have peace instead of fear. Erase the words you wrote. Then write this verse in the exact same spot!

Are you mad at anyone right now? Grab a pen and paper and write down this verse while thinking of the person you're angry with. Then take a deep breath in, and as you breathe out, ask God to help you forgive this person and let go of your anger.

Read about ten of God's commandments for his people in Deuteronomy 5:6-21. Which one of these is the hardest for you to obey? God doesn't give us commandments to try to make life harder. He gives them to make our lives better! God created you, and he knows what's *best* for you.

God keeps his promises, and he always tells the truth. Ask your parents, your Sunday school teacher, or another trusted adult about a time they've seen God keep a promise from the Bible. How has that promise impacted their life?

You must love the Lord your God with all your heart, all your soul, and all your strength.

Deuteronomy 6:5

Give generously to the poor, not grudgingly, for the Lord your God will bless you in everything you do.

Deuteronomy 15:10

The Lord your God will change your heart and the hearts of all your descendants, so that you will love him with all your heart and soul and so you may live!

Deuteronomy 30:6

This is my command—be strong and courageous! Do not be afraid or discouraged. For the Lord your God is with you wherever you go.

Joshua 1:9

Put this verse into practice: start a giving jar! Whenever you earn money, put part of it into the jar. When you see a need, use the money to help. Maybe a missionary visits your church or a neighbor needs money for groceries. Whatever God puts before you, you'll be ready!

Write this verse on a piece of paper. Read it out loud a few times. Then take another piece of paper and cover up different parts of the verse, trying to say the covered parts without peeking. Keep going until you can remember the entire verse.

This verse reminds us that God is with us wherever we go—and he helps us to be brave. Choose an exercise (push-ups, jumping jacks, etc.), and do ten repetitions three times. In between each set of ten repetitions, read this verse and thank God for helping you to be strong and courageous.

Sometimes our hearts are filled with fear, anger, or jealousy. But God can change our hearts! Grab a pen and paper, pretending the paper is your heart. (You can even cut it into a heart shape if you want.) Now write down what you think God wants to fill your heart with, and pray that he would do it.

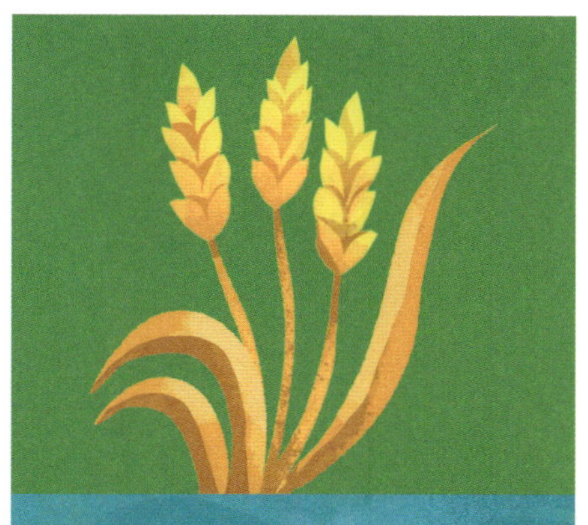

Don't ask me to leave you and turn back. Wherever you go, I will go; wherever you live, I will live. Your people will be my people, and your God will be my God.

Ruth 1:16

Don't judge by his appearance or height, for I have rejected him. The Lord doesn't see things the way you see them. People judge by outward appearance, but the Lord looks at the heart.

1 Samuel 16:7

Observe the requirements of the Lord your God, and follow all his ways. Keep the decrees, commands, regulations, and laws written in the Law of Moses so that you will be successful in all you do and wherever you go.

1 Kings 2:3

Praise the Lord who has given rest to his people Israel, just as he promised. Not one word has failed of all the wonderful promises he gave through his servant Moses.

1 Kings 8:56

What if you got a present wrapped in fancy paper and bows, but there was a moldy sandwich inside? Yuck! We usually notice the outside of a person first, but the inside is what matters most. Write this verse on a piece of paper, and list some of the inner qualities God wants us to have.

Read this verse out loud with a friend or family member. Then check out the feature about Ruth and Naomi on page 331 in the *Go Bible*. Read the verse out loud again and talk together about what being faithful to others can look like in your own life.

Take a look back at God's promises to Israel in Exodus 6:6-8. Write down how the Israelites might have felt when they were in slavery. Then draw a picture of the people resting in their own land because God kept his promise! What promises has God kept to you? Check out Proverbs 3:5-6 and 1 John 1:9 if you need ideas.

King David gave these instructions to his son Solomon based on a lifetime of experience. Think about the times when you've obeyed God. Write down or draw a picture of three examples from your own life and post them somewhere to remind you to always follow God.

If my people who are called by my name will humble themselves and pray and seek my face and turn from their wicked ways, I will hear from heaven and will forgive their sins and restore their land.

2 Chronicles 7:14

Listen, all you people of Judah and Jerusalem! Listen, King Jehoshaphat! This is what the Lord says: Do not be afraid! Don't be discouraged by this mighty army, for the battle is not yours, but God's.

2 Chronicles 20:15

You alone are the Lord. You made the skies and the heavens and all the stars. You made the earth and the seas and everything in them. You preserve them all, and the angels of heaven worship you.

Nehemiah 9:6

If you keep quiet at a time like this, deliverance and relief for the Jews will arise from some other place, but you and your relatives will die. Who knows if perhaps you were made queen for just such a time as this?

Esther 4:14

Sometimes it's hard not to be afraid, even when you're trying to trust God. Singing songs of praise and thanks to God as the Israelites did is one great way to overcome fear. Try listening to some praise songs today. Make a list of your favorites so you can sing them next time you're afraid.

Sometimes we make bad choices. When that happens, God wants us to tell him we're sorry and ask for his help. Today, take a few minutes to read this verse and talk with God about what's going on in your life. Is there anything you need to apologize for or ask him to help you with?

In this verse, Mordecai encourages Esther by reminding her that God has a purpose for her. Do you know someone who's having a hard time or facing a difficult decision? Ask God how you can encourage them this week. Maybe you could write them a note or pray for them.

God has placed some amazing creations in the skies, on the earth, and in the seas! Just think of all the constellations in the sky, the beautiful flowers on the earth, and the gigantic whales in the sea. After you read this verse, ask an adult to help you look up some fun facts about God's wonderful creation in the sky, earth, or sea. Share what you learn with a friend!

As for me, I know that my
Redeemer lives,
and he will stand upon the
earth at last.

Job 19:25

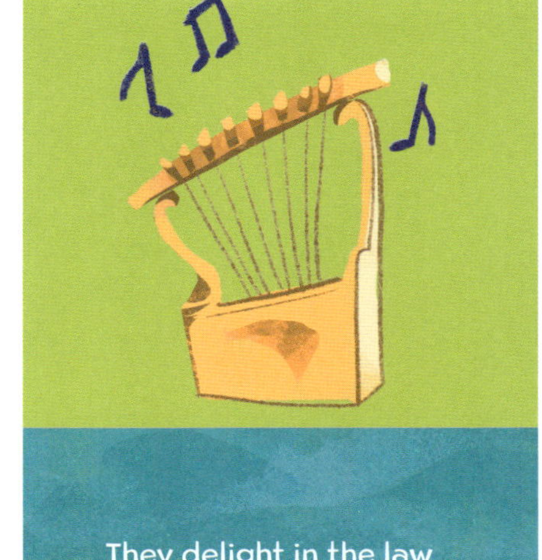

They delight in the law
of the Lord,
meditating on it day
and night.

Psalm 1:2

I will thank the Lord
because he is just;
I will sing praise to the
name of the Lord Most
High.

Psalm 7:17

I know the Lord is always
with me.
I will not be shaken, for he
is right beside me.

Psalm 16:8

Tomorrow, when you wake up, pray before you even get out of bed! At night, read Psalm 1 and pray right before you go to sleep. Thank God that we can learn from him by reading his words in the Bible.

Job wanted God to defend him and explain his suffering. We can trust God to advocate for us, too. God showed everyone his power to redeem (which means to set free) by sending Jesus to die for us. After you memorize this verse, twist some pipe cleaners into the shape of a cross to remind you of God's power and love.

After you memorize this verse, place a sheet of paper in front of a fan and turn the fan on. What happens? Now hold the paper in front of the fan with both hands. God is like those two hands, keeping you from being shaken in hard times.

Psalm 7 was originally meant to be a song! Try coming up with a tune for verse 17. Sing it out loud until you have it memorized. Then sing it with your eyes closed and your hands raised high in praise to God.

May the words of my mouth
and the meditation
of my heart
be pleasing to you,
O Lord, my rock
and my redeemer.

Psalm 19:14

The Lord is my shepherd;
I have all that I need.
He lets me rest in green
meadows;
he leads me beside
peaceful streams.

Psalm 23:1-2

He renews my strength.
He guides me along right
paths,
bringing honor to his name.

Psalm 23:3

Even when I walk
through the darkest valley,
I will not be afraid,
for you are close beside me.
Your rod and your staff
protect and comfort me.

Psalm 23:4

Memorize Psalm 23! Draw a sheep at the top of a piece of paper. Each time you memorize one verse from this chapter, glue a cotton ball onto your sheep and write the verse you just memorized below your drawing. Hang your sheep on the wall to remind you of your progress!

Go outside and find a unique rock. With a permanent marker, write "Psalm 19:14" on the rock. Place it on your nightstand or your dresser—somewhere you are sure to see it often. Whenever you do, think about this verse, and ask God to help you please him with your words and thoughts.

Memorize Psalm 23! Draw a sheep at the top of a piece of paper. Each time you memorize one verse from this chapter, glue a cotton ball onto your sheep and write the verse you just memorized below your drawing. Hang your sheep on the wall to remind you of your progress!

Memorize Psalm 23! Draw a sheep at the top of a piece of paper. Each time you memorize one verse from this chapter, glue a cotton ball onto your sheep and write the verse you just memorized below your drawing. Hang your sheep on the wall to remind you of your progress!

You prepare a feast for me
in the presence of my
enemies.
You honor me by anointing
my head with oil.

Psalm 23:5

Surely your goodness and
unfailing love will pursue me
all the days of my life,
and I will live in the house of
the Lord forever.

Psalm 23:6

Be strong and courageous,
all you who put your hope in
the Lord!

Psalm 31:24

The Lord is close to the
brokenhearted;
he rescues those whose
spirits are crushed.

Psalm 34:18

Memorize Psalm 23! Draw a sheep at the top of a piece of paper. Each time you memorize one verse from this chapter, glue a cotton ball onto your sheep and write the verse you just memorized below your drawing. Hang your sheep on the wall to remind you of your progress!

Memorize Psalm 23! Draw a sheep at the top of a piece of paper. Each time you memorize one verse from this chapter, glue a cotton ball onto your sheep and write the verse you just memorized below your drawing. Hang your sheep on the wall to remind you of your progress!

Ask a trusted adult to share with you how God helped them through a painful time. Together, crumple and tear up some sheets of construction paper. Glue the pieces into the shape of a heart on top of another sheet of paper. Write this verse around the heart as a reminder that God heals and comforts us when we're sad.

Create a certificate to remind yourself to be strong and courageous. Write this verse on a piece of paper, then write underneath it, "I, [insert your name], place my hope in God. Because of that, I am strong and courageous." Decorate your paper to make it look official!

Be still, and know that I am
God!
I will be honored by every
nation.
I will be honored
throughout the world.

Psalm 46:10

Create in me a clean heart,
O God.
Renew a loyal spirit
within me.

Psalm 51:10

When I am afraid,
I will put my trust in you.

Psalm 56:3

May the nations praise you,
O God.
Yes, may all the nations
praise you.
Let the whole world sing for joy,
because you govern the
nations with justice
and guide the people of the
whole world.

Psalm 67:3-4

Volunteer to help wash the dishes tonight. As you scrub and rinse each dish, pay attention to how it changes from dirty to clean. Ask God to clean your heart in the same way. Memorize this verse, and thank God for making a clean heart possible.

Find a quiet place with sunlight in your house, or if the weather is good, go outside. Then sit on the ground or floor and close your eyes. Let the sun shine down upon you. Be still and be quiet. Count to sixty in your mind. Then recite this verse. Increase your time of silence from one minute to five minutes. Is it hard, or is it easy to be still?

Ask an adult which nation in the world is going through a difficult time right now. Together, make a list of the ways you can pray for the people in that nation. Ask God to guide these people, protect them, and show them his love. Pray through your list together, and consider making it a regular habit.

Write down a list of things that scare you. Put it inside an envelope labeled "Trust." Slip that envelope inside a larger one with this verse written on it. Thank God that he is large enough to handle it all. Keep the envelope as a reminder to put your trust in him.

A single day in your courts
is better than a thousand
anywhere else!
I would rather be a
gatekeeper in the house
of my God
than live the good life in
the homes of the wicked.

Psalm 84:10

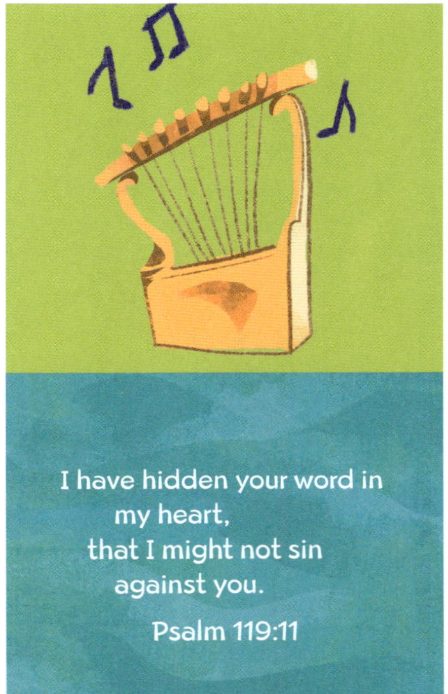

I have hidden your word in
my heart,
that I might not sin
against you.

Psalm 119:11

Your word is a lamp to guide
my feet
and a light for my path.

Psalm 119:105

Give thanks to the Lord,
for he is good!
His faithful love endures
forever.

Psalm 136:1

What's a sin you have a hard time resisting? Speaking unkind words? Disobeying your parents? Telling lies? The Bible is a powerful tool to help you fight whatever sin you struggle with. Memorize this Bible verse to remind yourself of the power of God's Word.

After memorizing this verse, find a friend or sibling for a fun game of Would You Rather? Here's an example: "Would you rather be able to fly or turn invisible?" Every time you play this game, remember that being with God is better than anything else in the world.

Each day, write down one thing you are thankful for on a slip of paper and drop it into a jar. Invite your family and friends to write down what they are thankful for too. After a few weeks, read through the papers together, thanking God for his faithful love.

Write each word of this verse on its own sheet of paper. Line up the papers on the floor to make a path—then turn out the lights! Use a flashlight to guide you down the path, reading the verse as you go. God guides you with his Word just like a flashlight in the dark.

Thank you for making me so wonderfully complex! Your workmanship is marvelous—how well I know it.

Psalm 139:14

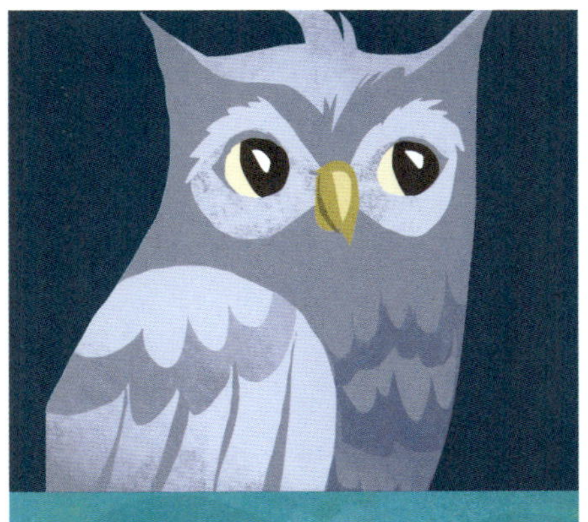

Trust in the Lord with all your heart;
do not depend on your own understanding.
Seek his will in all you do,
and he will show you which path to take.

Proverbs 3:5-6

We can make our plans, but the Lord determines our steps.

Proverbs 16:9

Two people are better off than one, for they can help each other succeed.

Ecclesiastes 4:9

Memorize these verses by setting them to music. Use the rhythm of the words to create a tune. Repeat the song over and over until you know it by heart. Then sing it for your family!

After you memorize this verse, draw a picture of yourself. List the things that make you different from your family members or friends, even if you don't understand why those differences exist. Ask God to help you understand what you need to know about the way he designed you, and thank him for his marvelous work!

With a parent's permission, put a penny in a plastic cup and hang the cup from a dry spaghetti noodle supported between two boxes. How many pennies can one noodle hold? How many pennies can a bundle of spaghetti noodles hold? When you work with others, you can accomplish things that would have been impossible alone!

In the morning, write down your plans for the day. At the end of the day, write or draw what actually happened. How does it compare to what you expected? Did anything surprise you? Read this verse and ask God to help you trust him when things don't turn out the way you planned.

A child is born to us,
a son is given to us.
The government will
rest on his shoulders.
And he will be called:
Wonderful Counselor,
Mighty God,
Everlasting Father,
Prince of Peace.

Isaiah 9:6

You will keep in perfect peace
all who trust in you,
all whose thoughts are
fixed on you!

Isaiah 26:3

Those who trust in the Lord
will find new strength.
They will soar high on wings
like eagles.
They will run and not grow
weary.
They will walk and not faint.

Isaiah 40:31

I hold you by your right
hand—
I, the Lord your God.
And I say to you,
"Don't be afraid. I am here
to help you."

Isaiah 41:13

Have you ever played a game like beanbag toss or darts? These activities require focus. In the same way, God wants us to focus our attention on him because remembering his power and goodness brings us peace. Practice your concentration skills by playing a game that requires focus. In between turns, recite this verse.

Make a crown out of construction paper and write the titles listed in these verses around the crown. Then memorize the verses one line at a time. This is just one of many prophecies in Isaiah that point ahead to the Messiah, Jesus.

Trace your right hand on a piece of construction paper, then cut it out. Now write this verse across the paper hand and put the hand on your refrigerator. If someone in your family is fearful or anxious, remind them of this verse. God is always here to help us.

Eagles eventually learn to soar thousands of feet in the air by learning from their parents' examples. After you memorize this verse, ask your parents or another trusted adult to tell you about a time when God provided the strength they needed to soar above life's challenges.

"The mountains may move
and the hills disappear,
but even then my faithful love
for you will remain.
My covenant of blessing
will never be broken,"
says the Lord, who has
mercy on you.

Isaiah 54:10

This is what the Lord says:
"Stop at the crossroads and
look around.
Ask for the old, godly way,
and walk in it.
Travel its path, and you will
find rest for your souls.
But you reply, 'No, that's
not the road we want!'"

Jeremiah 6:16

Blessed are those who trust
in the Lord
and have made the
Lord their hope and
confidence.

Jeremiah 17:7

"I know the plans I have for
you," says the Lord. "They
are plans for good and not
for disaster, to give you
a future and a hope."

Jeremiah 29:11

After you memorize this verse, draw a map of your neighborhood and circle the crossroads. While we don't have a map showing every turn our lives will take, did you know that God provides markers to guide us? The Bible, prayer, and wise advice are some of the markers he uses.

It would take a pretty big earthquake to move a mountain, wouldn't it? God's love for you is so big that not even the biggest "earthquake" in your life could make him stop loving you. As a reminder of this promise, glue a rock to a piece of cardboard, then write or paint this verse underneath it.

Think about your favorite story. When you read it for the first time, did you know how it was going to turn out? God is the Author of your life. Every morning for a week, recite this verse aloud and thank God for the good plans he has for your story, even though you don't know them yet.

Read Jeremiah 17:58. Whom does Jeremiah compare to shrubs in the wilderness, and whom does he compare to trees by a river? With an adult's help, look up images of the Dead Sea and the Jordan River. What do you notice about the plants near them? Print out a couple of images, and write verse 7 beneath them.

The faithful love of the Lord
never ends!
His mercies never cease.
Great is his faithfulness;
his mercies begin afresh
each morning.

Lamentations 3:22-23

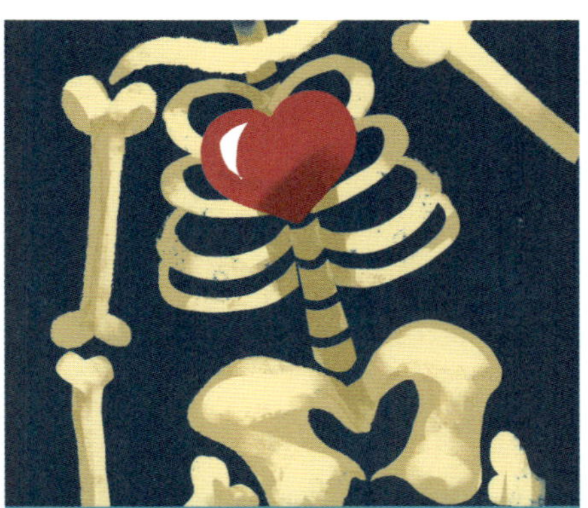

I will give you a new heart,
and I will put a new spirit in
you. I will take out your stony,
stubborn heart and give you
a tender, responsive heart.

Ezekiel 36:26

Praise the name of God
forever and ever,
for he has all wisdom
and power.

Daniel 2:20

So now, come back to
your God.
Act with love and justice,
and always depend on him.

Hosea 12:6

Find two clear, disposable cups. Fill one with good dirt. Fill the other with rocks. Plant seeds in each cup, water them, and watch what happens. God wants to transform us so we love and serve him, but often our hearts are as hard as those rocks. Thankfully, God can soften any heart, making it like the good dirt!

Cut out a long strip of paper. On one side write *mercy*, and on the other write *love*. Then tape the narrow ends together, creating a ring of paper. Loops are never-ending, just like God's faithful mercy and love. Put the loop next to your bed to remind yourself of this verse each morning and night.

Coming back to God means asking for forgiveness. It also means asking for his help to love others and treat them fairly. Is there anything you need to tell God you're sorry for? Ask him to help you act with love and justice—and to help you depend on him, just as this verse says.

When have you seen examples of God's wisdom and power? Write or draw a list! Maybe you've been amazed by an animal or plant God created. Or maybe God provided something your family needed. Spend some time praising God for each item on your list, and write this verse at the top.

"Don't tear your clothing
   in your grief,
   but tear your hearts instead."
Return to the Lord your God,
   for he is merciful and
   compassionate,
slow to get angry and filled
   with unfailing love.
He is eager to relent and not
   punish.

Joel 2:13

Instead, I want to see a
   mighty flood of justice,
   an endless river of righteous
   living.

Amos 5:24

No, O people, the Lord has
   told you what is good,
   and this is what he requires
   of you:
to do what is right,
   to love mercy,
   and to walk humbly
   with your God.

Micah 6:8

The Lord is good,
   a strong refuge when
   trouble comes.
He is close to those who
   trust in him.

Nahum 1:7

What would an endless river look like? It would go on and on forever. It would never pour into a lake or ocean, and its source of water would be unlimited. Design a river out of modeling clay or construction paper while repeating this verse out loud to help you remember it. Imagine that your river has no end!

Memorize this verse by writing its words in random order on a piece of paper and drawing a line to connect them in the right order. Repeat the verse to yourself whenever you feel guilty or ashamed, and allow God's mercy, compassion, and love to fill you up.

You go to a refuge because you trust that you will be safe there. It's similar to a fort. Build a pillow fort and make a banner for the entrance with this verse on it! Every time you enter your fort, remember God's goodness and protection.

Write "Do right," "Love mercy," and "Walk humbly" on note cards, and ask an adult what they mean. Tape the note cards to your bathroom mirror, and read them every morning and every night. Each time you read them, ask God to help you do them!

Look at the proud!
They trust in themselves,
and their lives are
crooked.
But the righteous will live by
their faithfulness to God.

Habakkuk 2:4

The Lord your God is living
among you.
He is a mighty savior.
He will take delight in you
with gladness.
With his love, he will calm
all your fears.
He will rejoice over you with
joyful songs.

Zephaniah 3:17

Don't scheme against each
other. Stop your love of
telling lies that you swear
are the truth. I hate all these
things, says the Lord.

Zechariah 8:17

The Lord is compassionate
and merciful,
slow to get angry and filled
with unfailing love.

Psalm 103:8

Next time you're going into a scary or stressful situation, bring your Bible with you and have this verse marked. Read it out loud or in your head and thank God for loving you and being with you. Be quiet for a moment and imagine God delighting in you, calming you, and rejoicing over you.

Put on a blindfold and try to walk in a straight line. Now try it without the blindfold. When we don't trust God to guide us, it's kind of like having a blindfold on. Our path will be crooked! But when we turn to God for direction, he'll steer us the right way.

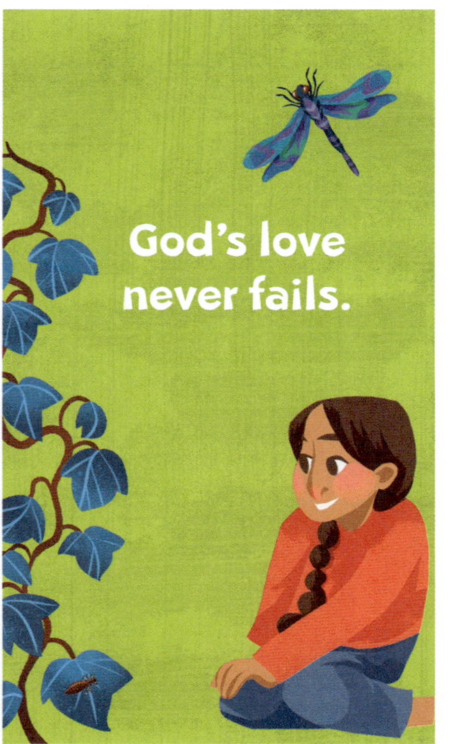

Tricking someone else (even if it seems like a harmless practical joke) and telling lies lead to trouble. Instead, plan a way to encourage someone today. Think of something kind you can do for that person, then tell them something you truly like about them.

You go before me and
follow me.
You place your hand of
blessing on my head.

Psalm 139:5

How precious are your thoughts
about me, O God.
They cannot be numbered!
I can't even count them;
they outnumber the grains
of sand!
And when I wake up,
you are still with me!

Psalm 139:17-18

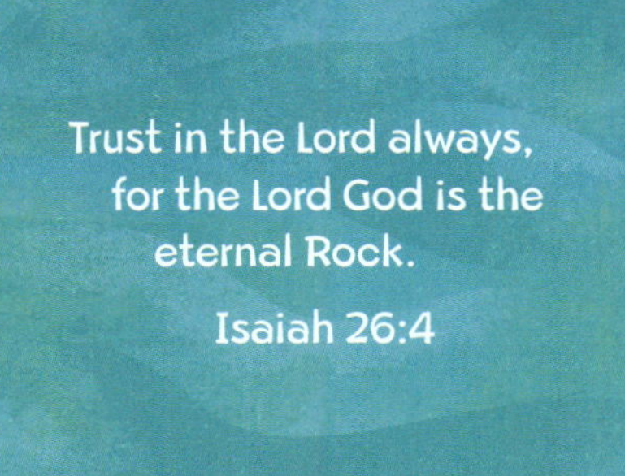

Trust in the Lord always,
for the Lord God is the
eternal Rock.

Isaiah 26:4

Don't be afraid, for I am
with you.
Don't be discouraged, for I
am your God.
I will strengthen you and
help you.
I will hold you up with my
victorious right hand.

Isaiah 41:10

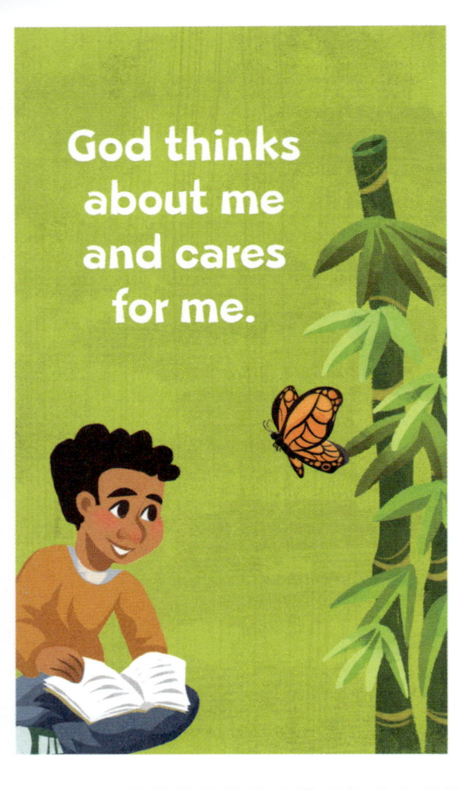

God thinks about me and cares for me.

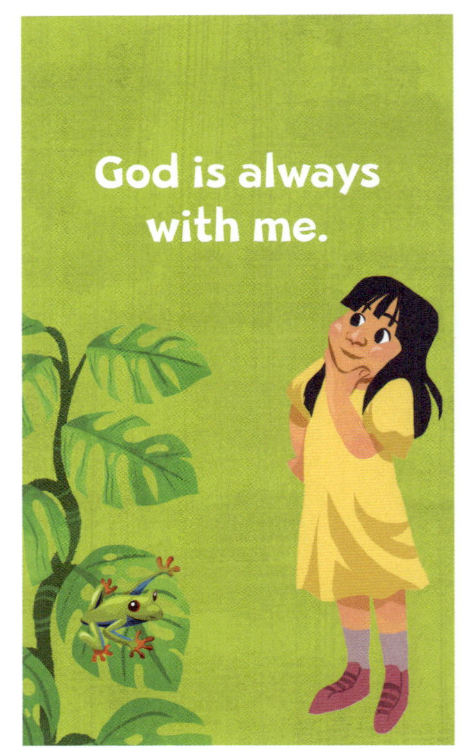

God is always with me.

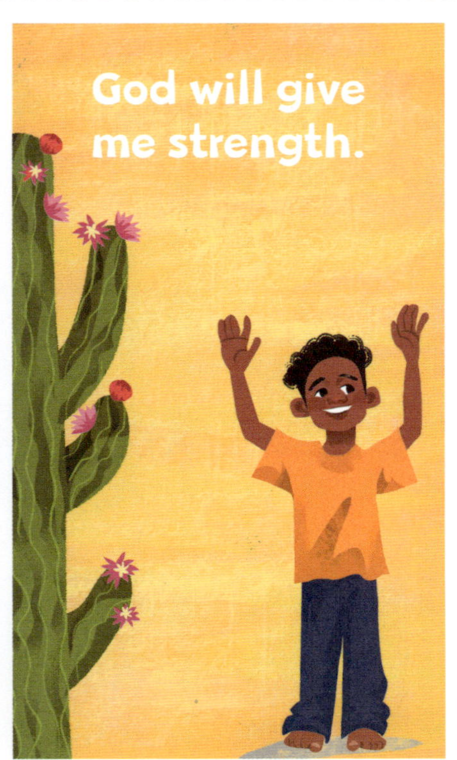

God will give me strength.

God is as trustworthy as an unbreakable rock.

She will have a son, and you are to name him Jesus, for he will save his people from their sins.

Matthew 1:21

Don't worry about tomorrow, for tomorrow will bring its own worries. Today's trouble is enough for today.

Matthew 6:34

If you cling to your life, you will lose it; but if you give up your life for me, you will find it.

Matthew 10:39

Come to me, all of you who are weary and carry heavy burdens, and I will give you rest.

Matthew 11:28

Have you ever seen a worried tree? Of course not! Trees don't worry, and neither should you. Find a big leaf outside, then put that leaf in your Bible to bookmark this verse. Next time you feel worried, turn back to this verse and read it to yourself.

God specifically chose Jesus' name, which means "The Lord saves," to reveal the reason Jesus was born. Through Jesus, God saves us from being separated from him by our sin. Memorize this verse, then ask your parents or guardians what your name means!

Carry a stack of books around your house and repeat this verse to yourself until you're tired. Then put the books away and notice how good it feels to set down that load. Is anything weighing you down on the inside? Tell Jesus about it, and picture handing it over to him. He will take care of it!

God wants us to live our lives for him and honor him with everything we do. When we ask for his help to do that, what we value will change. We will put Jesus first and care about following him more than anything else. Write down this verse today. Then write some ways you want to live for Jesus.

He asked them, "But who do you say I am?"

Simon Peter answered, "You are the Messiah, the Son of the living God."

Matthew 16:15-16

Let the children come to me. Don't stop them! For the Kingdom of Heaven belongs to those who are like these children.

Matthew 19:14

"You must love the Lord your God with all your heart, all your soul, and all your mind." This is the first and greatest commandment. A second is equally important: "Love your neighbor as yourself."

Matthew 22:37-39

Go and make disciples of all the nations, baptizing them in the name of the Father and the Son and the Holy Spirit.

Matthew 28:19

Jesus is never too busy for you, and he'll never turn away. Design an invitation from Jesus addressed to you for any time, any place! Write this verse at the bottom. Grab the invitation whenever you feel unworthy to talk with Jesus as a reminder that he wants you to come to him no matter what.

"Who do you say I am?" Jesus asks each one of us this question. If you can honestly declare like Peter that Jesus is the Son of God, then tell Jesus that and thank him for showing you who he is. If you still have questions, that's okay. Bring them to an adult you trust who knows Jesus.

Do you have a globe or a map? Look for a place that's far away from where you live. Next, find somewhere that's not marked with any cities. People live in nearly every part of the world. Today, pray for people in areas of the world where Jesus isn't known— that they would hear about him and choose to follow him.

Understanding what you're supposed to do is difficult sometimes, isn't it? Thankfully, Jesus simplified things for us in these verses. Write them on an index card and carry it in your backpack. Next time you don't know what to do, read the card and decide how you can show your love for God and others.

A voice from heaven said, "You are my dearly loved Son, and you bring me great joy."

Mark 1:11

He sat down, called the twelve disciples over to him, and said, "Whoever wants to be first must take last place and be the servant of everyone else."

Mark 9:35

The Savior—yes, the Messiah, the Lord—has been born today in Bethlehem, the city of David!

Luke 2:11

He asked them, "Where is your faith?"

The disciples were terrified and amazed. "Who is this man?" they asked each other. "When he gives a command, even the wind and waves obey him!"

Luke 8:25

Make a list of ways you can put others first today. For example, you could let someone go ahead of you in the lunch line, help a friend with their homework, or do a sibling's chore for them. Do as many things on the list as you can, and see what happens!

Have you made the commitment to give up living life your way and to live for God as his child? If you have but you haven't told others, talk to your parents and pastor about baptism or taking the next step. Then memorize this verse: the words God spoke after Jesus' baptism.

Fill your kitchen sink with water. Then use a spoon to make some waves. When you stop moving the spoon, the waves stop too, right? When Jesus told the wind and waves to stop, they obeyed. Jesus has authority over waves and wind because he created them. Today, thank Jesus that he's in control of every part of creation.

Get a piece of paper and some crayons or colored pencils. Draw what you think the scene looked like when Jesus was born in Bethlehem. Then, on the back of the picture, write this verse. Hang the picture somewhere for everyone to see.

Everyone who asks, receives.
Everyone who seeks, finds.
And to everyone who knocks,
the door will be opened.

Luke 11:10

Wherever your treasure
is, there the desires of
your heart will also be.

Luke 12:34

In the same way, there
is joy in the presence of
God's angels when even
one sinner repents.

Luke 15:10

If you are faithful in little
things, you will be faithful
in large ones. But if you are
dishonest in little things,
you won't be honest with
greater responsibilities.

Luke 16:10

Write the word *treasure* and today's date on an envelope. Then, on a piece of paper, write a list of the most valuable things in your life. Put the list in the envelope, and tuck the envelope in your Bible. A year from now, open the envelope and see if what you value has changed. Remember that everything on the list is a gift from God!

Start a prayer journal! In a notebook, write down your prayer requests and the date you start praying about them. Then record when and how God answers. Be prepared for God's answer to look different from what you expected, and even if that answer is a no, remember that God knows what is best for you.

After you memorize this verse, ask God to give you the strength to focus on what you already have instead of just wanting more. For example, God can help you develop the self-control to take care of the responsibilities your parents have already given you before you ask for more privileges. He loves to help us grow!

Have you done something wrong recently? Do you need to ask God to forgive you? Do it, and then leave all shame in the past as you enjoy his forgiveness! Make some homemade confetti out of paper, and celebrate with God over your healed and restored relationship.

What is impossible for people is possible with God.

Luke 18:27

In the beginning the Word already existed. The Word was with God, and the Word was God. He existed in the beginning with God. God created everything through him, and nothing was created except through him.

John 1:1-3

To all who believed him and accepted him, he gave the right to become children of God.

John 1:12

This is how God loved the world: He gave his one and only Son, so that everyone who believes in him will not perish but have eternal life.

John 3:16

Fold construction paper in half to make a little booklet. Write these verses on the inner lefthand side. Then go read Genesis 1. On the inner right-hand side of the booklet, write or draw all the things God created in Genesis 1. Draw a cross on the outside of the booklet to remind you that Jesus, the Word, has existed from the very beginning.

Bad news—it's impossible for you to live up to God's standards on your own. But there's good news too. Jesus has paid the price for you to receive forgiveness and enter God's Kingdom! Write this verse on a sticky note and put it on your bathroom mirror. Every day, thank God for his amazing gift.

Find a friend or family member and make up actions together to go with this verse. Say the verse out loud as you do the actions. Keep practicing until you have memorized this truth about God sending his Son for us— no peeking!

Jesus offers you the opportunity to become a son or daughter of God! All you have to do is believe in Jesus and accept his gift of forgiveness and new life. If you've done that, congratulations! Design a certificate with this verse on it to remind you of your adoption into God's family.

Jesus said to the people who believed in him, "You are truly my disciples if you remain faithful to my teachings. And you will know the truth, and the truth will set you free."

John 8:31-32

I am the resurrection and the life. Anyone who believes in me will live, even after dying.

John 11:25

I am giving you a new commandment: Love each other. Just as I have loved you, you should love each other. Your love for one another will prove to the world that you are my disciples.

John 13:34-35

I am the way, the truth, and the life. No one can come to the Father except through me.

John 14:6

Create a timeline to demonstrate that death isn't the end for people who love Jesus. Draw a mark on the left-hand side of your timeline to represent your birth, and make another mark toward the middle to represent the end of your life. Underneath the rest of the timeline, write, "Eternal life with Jesus!"

Jesus is the truth, and he wants to lead you to freedom from sin. After you memorize this verse, ask a family member to wrap you up in toilet paper. As you break out of the toilet paper, remember how Jesus has set you free!

There is only one way to God: believing that Jesus is God's Son and that his perfect life, death, and resurrection bridged the gap between sinful humans and our holy God! Design a maze and write Jesus' name at every correct turn. Sketch yourself at the entrance to the maze, and draw a line through the maze to reach God at the end.

What have you learned about love from Jesus' example in the book of John? Write a few things you've learned on small pieces of paper, and put all the papers in a jar. Each day, select one and ask Jesus to help you love people in a similar way. Thank him for helping you become more like him!

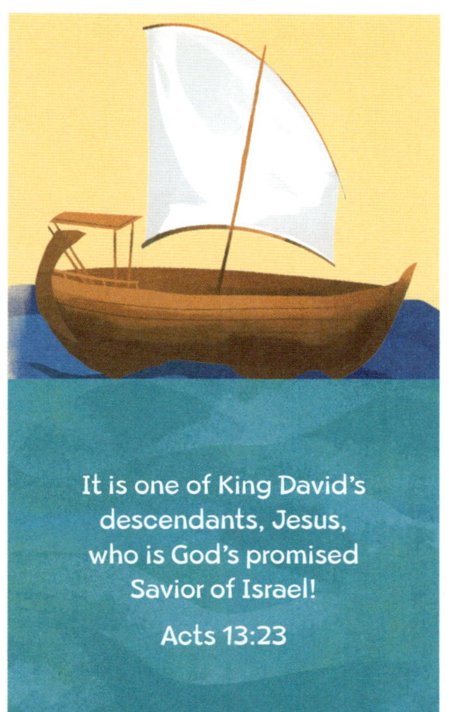

It is one of King David's
descendants, Jesus,
who is God's promised
Savior of Israel!

Acts 13:23

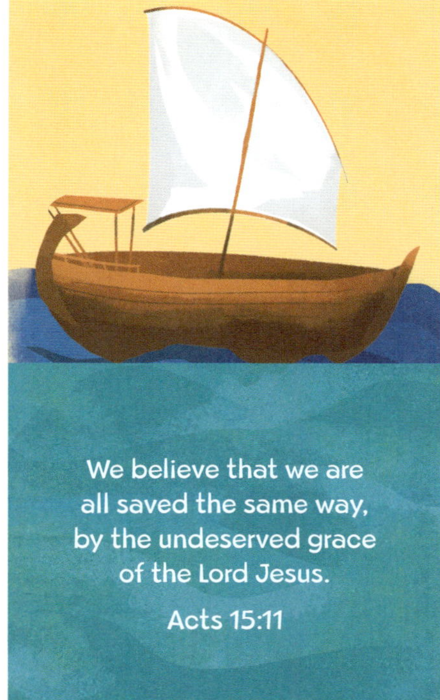

We believe that we are
all saved the same way,
by the undeserved grace
of the Lord Jesus.

Acts 15:11

I am not ashamed of this
Good News about Christ.
It is the power of God at
work, saving everyone who
believes—the Jew first
and also the Gentile.

Romans 1:16

This Good News tells us how
God makes us right in his
sight. This is accomplished
from start to finish by
faith. As the Scriptures say,
"It is through faith that a
righteous person has life."

Romans 1:17

Draw a picture or collect some items as a reminder of times someone showed you grace (which means they gave you a gift or did something nice for you even though you didn't deserve it). Next time you start to get mad at some-one, take a deep breath and think about this verse and the grace you've received. How can you show grace to others?

Read the list of Jesus' family members in Matthew 1. Then draw a chain connecting the generations between David and Jesus. Write Acts 13:23 at the end as a reminder that God will keep all his promises—just like he kept his promise to send Jesus, our Savior.

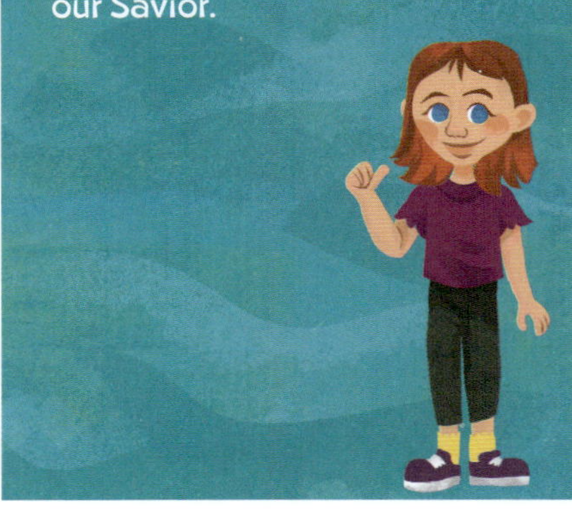

Ask a trusted Christian adult to memorize Romans 1:16-17 with you. Then brainstorm together how to share the Good News clearly with others, and pray that God would give you both oppor-tunities to talk about Jesus with the people in your lives.

Ask a trusted Christian adult to memorize Romans 1:16-17 with you. Then brainstorm together how to share the Good News clearly with others, and pray that God would give you both opportunities to talk about Jesus with the people in your lives.

Everyone has sinned; we all fall short of God's glorious standard. Yet God, in his grace, freely makes us right in his sight. He did this through Christ Jesus when he freed us from the penalty for our sins.

Romans 3:23-24

God showed his great love for us by sending Christ to die for us while we were still sinners.

Romans 5:8

We know that God causes everything to work together for the good of those who love God and are called according to his purpose for them.

Romans 8:28

If you openly declare that Jesus is Lord and believe in your heart that God raised him from the dead, you will be saved.

Romans 10:9

It's easy to love people who love us back. But God loves us even when we don't love him. Do you know someone who hasn't been very nice to you? Think of something kind you can do for them this week. If they ask why you did it, tell them about God's love and share this verse with them.

Turn on the faucet in your bathroom sink and open your hand under the stream of water. When God sent Jesus to die for you, he poured out his grace—just like the water flowing from the faucet. Write this passage on a note card and tape it near the sink so you'll remember it next time you wash your hands.

Do you believe that Jesus died and came back to life to make a way for you to be right with God? Do you want to dedicate your life to following him? Congratulations! You are part of God's family. Go share the good news with someone you trust, and look for ways to show your faith through your actions.

Ask a parent or guardian to help you find an Impressionist painting online. When you zoom in on an individual stroke of color in the painting, it may seem pointless. Together though, these strokes create a beautiful painting. Like a skilled artist, God uses each event in the lives of his children to create a masterpiece. Print out your favorite Impressionist painting to help you remember this verse.

Rejoice in our confident hope. Be patient in trouble, and keep on praying.

Romans 12:12

Accept each other just as Christ has accepted you so that God will be given glory.

Romans 15:7

We have received God's Spirit (not the world's spirit), so we can know the wonderful things God has freely given us.

1 Corinthians 2:12

The temptations in your life are no different from what others experience. And God is faithful. He will not allow the temptation to be more than you can stand. When you are tempted, he will show you a way out so that you can endure.

1 Corinthians 10:13

Find a dry-erase marker. Write this verse across a mirror. Then read it, erase a word, and say it again. Continue erasing words until none are left and you can recite the verse fully. Then put the verse into practice by showing patience and understanding to the people around you.

Think about what gives you confident hope in God. Now make up a melody to go along with this verse to help you memorize it! When you sing it, remember that God wants to give you guidance, strength, and comfort in difficult situations.

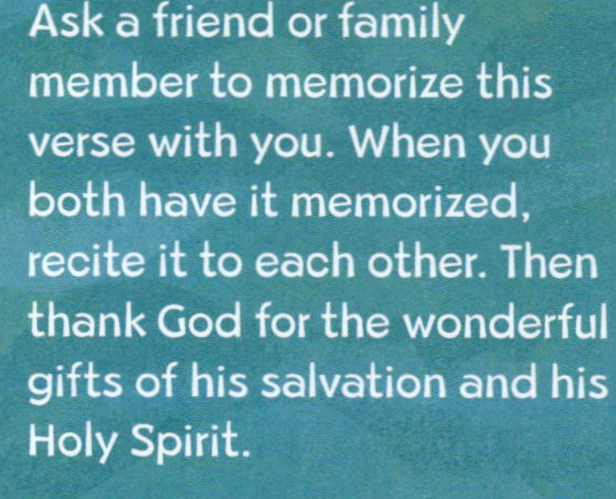

Sin can seem very appealing, and if you rely on your own strength, you will eventually fall into doing the wrong thing. But God says he will provide a way out. Think of a tempting situation you've faced, and say this verse as you imagine how you could run to God to escape that trap.

Ask a friend or family member to memorize this verse with you. When you both have it memorized, recite it to each other. Then thank God for the wonderful gifts of his salvation and his Holy Spirit.

Three things will last forever—
faith, hope, and love—and
the greatest of these is love.

1 Corinthians 13:13

Let me reveal to you a
wonderful secret. We will
not all die, but we will
all be transformed!

1 Corinthians 15:51

The Lord is the Spirit, and
wherever the Spirit of the
Lord is, there is freedom.

2 Corinthians 3:17

This means that anyone who
belongs to Christ has become
a new person. The old life is
gone; a new life has begun!

2 Corinthians 5:17

Gather several different types of seeds and take pictures of them. Then plant the seeds and watch them grow. How do the plants compare to the seeds? Even though people die and their bodies are buried like those seeds, new life will come one day. Jesus will return and give all Christians transformed bodies that will never get sick or die!

Once you've memorized this verse, try to describe the meaning of faith, hope, and love—and ask an older adult how they would define those words. Brainstorm some ways to live out faith, hope, and love this week, and don't forget to ask God for his help.

Grab some modeling clay and sculpt a dollar bill to represent a person who does whatever they want. Reshape that object into a heart, representing a person transformed by Christ. Believing in Jesus' great love for us gives us a whole new life.

Jesus took the penalty for our sin and made it possible for us to fully enter into the amazing freedom of a relationship with God! Cut or tear a piece of construction paper into a long rectangle. Use a marker to write this verse on it, and put it in your Bible as a bookmark.

Thank God for this gift too wonderful for words!

2 Corinthians 9:15

My old self has been crucified with Christ. It is no longer I who live, but Christ lives in me. So I live in this earthly body by trusting in the Son of God, who loved me and gave himself for me.

Galatians 2:20

The Holy Spirit produces this kind of fruit in our lives: love, joy, peace, patience, kindness, goodness, faithfulness, gentleness, and self-control. There is no law against these things!

Galatians 5:22-23

Let's not get tired of doing what is good. At just the right time we will reap a harvest of blessing if we don't give up.

Galatians 6:9

Learn this verse one sentence at a time. After you memorize each sentence, draw a picture that shows what it means to you: (sentence 1) your old self (before knowing Jesus); (sentence 2) Jesus living in you; (sentence 3) trusting in Jesus each day. Show the pictures to a friend or family member, and ask them to draw their own!

Read this verse silently. Then read it aloud. Read it silently again. Close your eyes and say as much as you can remember. Practice until you have this short verse sealed in your mind and heart. Try thinking of this verse every morning when you wake up, and thank God for his gift of grace.

Make a list of good things you can do for other people over the next month, and then look back at the end of the month. What happened? Did you make a new friend or grow in your relationship with God? Sometimes we won't see the results right away, but God promises that eventually our good work will produce blessings.

Paint a picture of some of your favorite kinds of fruit. Label them with the fruit of the Spirit from these verses. Do you see evidence of those character qualities in your life? Are any qualities of the Spirit's fruit harder for you? Ask the Holy Spirit to grow his good fruit in your life.

God saved you by his grace when you believed. And you can't take credit for this; it is a gift from God.

Ephesians 2:8

All glory to God, who is able, through his mighty power at work within us, to accomplish infinitely more than we might ask or think.

Ephesians 3:20

Let the Spirit renew your thoughts and attitudes. Put on your new nature, created to be like God— truly righteous and holy.

Ephesians 4:23-24

A final word: Be strong in the Lord and in his mighty power.

Ephesians 6:10

Write this verse down on a note card and read it each day for the next seven days. Then give the card to a family member and challenge them to memorize it too. Talk together about how you have seen God's power at work in your lives.

Sing this verse to the tune of "Row, Row, Row Your Boat" until you've got it memorized. Then get a couple of friends to sing it with you. Every time you sing it, praise God for the gift of his grace.

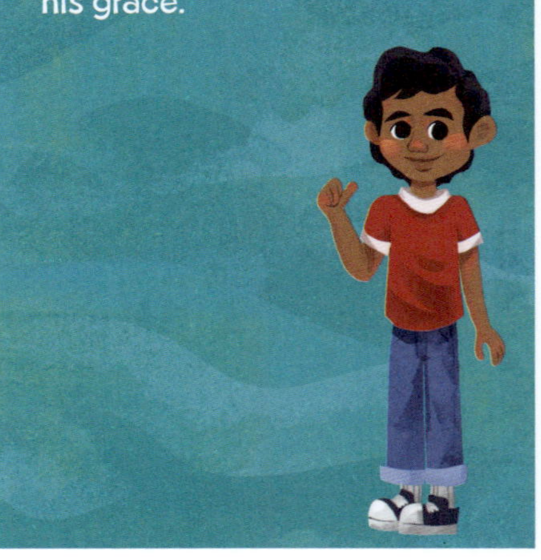

Make a suit of armor for a teddy bear, doll, or action figure. (Include every piece of armor mentioned in Ephesians 6:14-17.) Armor protects a person from receiving injuries they couldn't survive. When you go through hard times, rely on God's pres-ence, his Word, and the courage he gives you. He will enable you to get through anything.

A shower or bath washes away dirt, cleaning your physical body. But what about your thoughts and attitudes? Ask the Holy Spirit to renew your mind through reading your Bible, going on a prayer walk, or listening to worship music.

I am certain that God,
who began the good work
within you, will continue
his work until it is finally
finished on the day when
Christ Jesus returns.

Philippians 1:6

Don't look out only for your
own interests, but take an
interest in others, too.

Philippians 2:4

I can do everything through
Christ, who gives me strength.

Philippians 4:13

We speak as messengers
approved by God to be
entrusted with the Good
News. Our purpose is to
please God, not people.
He alone examines the
motives of our hearts.

1 Thessalonians 2:4

After you memorize this verse, look for ways to put others' needs above your own. Maybe you could use your free time to help your parents clean the house or mow the yard, play with your younger siblings, or call a grandparent. See if you can do one thing for someone else every day this week.

Spend some time working on something you love. How did you feel when you finished your work? Did you get distracted and forget to complete it? When you committed to following Jesus, God began his work to make you more and more like Jesus. Thank God that he doesn't get distracted—and that he will never give up on you.

Ask your parents or guardians for a stamped envelope, an index card, and the address of a relative or friend. Write this verse down on one side of the index card. On the other side, write a note to your relative or friend asking them to memorize this verse with you. Then mail it!

When life is hard, it can feel extra difficult to keep following God. But God doesn't expect you to do it alone. He will give you the strength to get through hard times. As you memorize this verse, strengthen your mind and body: try to do a push-up as you say each word out loud.

Always be joyful. Never stop praying. Be thankful in all circumstances, for this is God's will for you who belong to Christ Jesus.

1 Thessalonians 5:16-18

Don't let anyone think less of you because you are young. Be an example to all believers in what you say, in the way you live, in your love, your faith, and your purity.

1 Timothy 4:12

God has not given us a spirit of fear and timidity, but of power, love, and self-discipline.

2 Timothy 1:7

All Scripture is inspired by God and is useful to teach us what is true and to make us realize what is wrong in our lives. It corrects us when we are wrong and teaches us to do what is right.

2 Timothy 3:16

Once you've got this verse memorized, do jumping jacks while you recite it. Then ask God to help you remember that you don't have to wait to be an adult before you can be an example for him. You can start today, while you're young!

Get a blank piece of paper and write these verses at the top. Then write a list of the good things you notice in your life this week. How many can you find? Thank God for each thing as you think of it. You'll find yourself praying more and more frequently. You'll also find yourself becoming more thankful!

How do we know if something is true? One of the main ways God teaches us truth is through his written Word, the Bible. Is there something in your life you're struggling to understand the truth about? Memorize this verse and share it with a trusted adult. Ask them to help you find some other Bible verses or a Bible study on the issue you're struggling with.

Fear can hold you back from being everything God created you to be. As a Christian, God's Spirit is with you. He empowers you to tell people about Jesus through your words and actions, even when it's scary. Once you memorize this verse, make a list of the good things you can do as God helps you overcome your fear.

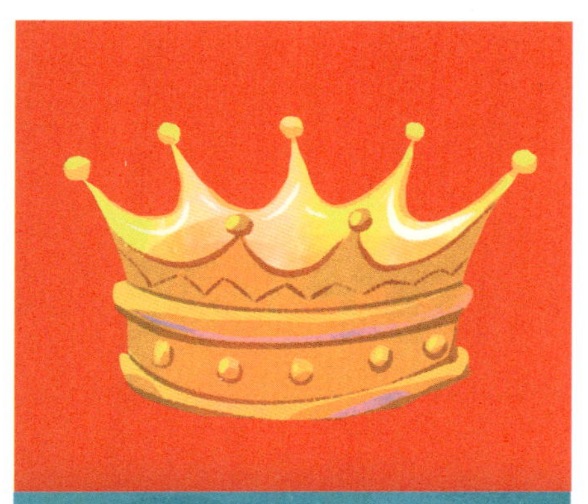

I have fought the good fight,
I have finished the race, and
I have remained faithful.

2 Timothy 4:7

Because of his grace he
made us right in his sight
and gave us confidence that
we will inherit eternal life.

Titus 3:7

Faith shows the reality
of what we hope for;
it is the evidence of
things we cannot see.

Hebrews 11:1

Jesus Christ is the same
yesterday, today, and forever.

Hebrews 13:8

Write this verse out on a sheet of paper. Then cut the verse into three equal sections. Put the pieces into a cup. Take out one of the sections and complete the verse by reciting the words that are missing. Repeat this a few times until you have the verse memorized.

Test how many laps you can run or walk around your yard or a park! Between each lap, pause and read this verse aloud a few times. Pray that God will give you the strength and dedication to run the race of the Christian life, especially when it's hard.

This verse is short, but it's strong. Anything in your life could change at any time—except for Jesus. He's the only one you can always trust and always rely on because he never changes. Memorize this verse so you can hold on to it no matter what happens.

You can feel your heart, you can hear your heart, but you can't see it. Yet you know it's there, and it makes your life possible. Confident faith does the same thing for the Christian life. You can't see it, but you need it in order to follow Jesus. Memorize this verse while placing your hand over your heart.

If you need wisdom, ask our generous God, and he will give it to you. He will not rebuke you for asking.

James 1:5

Don't repay evil for evil. Don't retaliate with insults when people insult you. Instead, pay them back with a blessing. That is what God has called you to do, and he will grant you his blessing.

1 Peter 3:9

Give all your worries and cares to God, for he cares about you.

1 Peter 5:7

If we confess our sins to him, he is faithful and just to forgive us our sins and to cleanse us from all wickedness.

1 John 1:9

On five slips of paper, write down this verse followed by a way you can be kind to someone. Start a "blessing bank" by saving the slips in a piggy bank or jar. When someone insults you and you want to pay them back, go to your blessing bank, take out a slip of paper, and do something kind for that person instead.

Seeing things with God's wisdom is kind of like putting on a new pair of glasses. God can help you understand how to respond wisely to a tough situation if you ask him. Before you memorize this verse, make a pair of glasses out of pipe cleaners. Put them on and repeat this verse to yourself, then ask God for the wisdom you need.

Ask a family member or friend to memorize this verse with you. Read it aloud to them. Then have them repeat it back to you. Do this again and again until you both have the verse memorized. Then pray together, thanking God for his forgiveness.

How heavy is your backpack? Could you carry more? You might think that you should carry some difficult and worrisome things alone. But God wants you to admit that your worries weigh you down and that you need his loving help. Imagine handing your backpack of worries to God while you memorize this verse.

We know what real love is because Jesus gave up his life for us. So we also ought to give up our lives for our brothers and sisters.

1 John 3:16

God showed how much he loved us by sending his one and only Son into the world so that we might have eternal life through him.

1 John 4:9

This is real love—not that we loved God, but that he loved us and sent his Son as a sacrifice to take away our sins.

1 John 4:10

Dear children, keep away from anything that might take God's place in your hearts.

1 John 5:21

Thank God for loving you long before you loved him. Once you've memorized 1 John 4:9-10, make a card for someone who's lonely or going through a hard time. (Ask a parent or guardian if you need ideas.) Write these verses on one side of the card, and write your own message on the other side.

Jesus' actions showed that his love is real. What do your actions show? What's something that you could give up to show love to a family member or friend? Memorize this verse so you can remember what Jesus gave up for you. Ask him to help you love others even when it's difficult.

Copy this verse onto a piece of paper and draw a heart underneath it. Inside the heart, draw or write some of the main things you love. Would you be able to focus more on God if you added or removed anything from your heart?

Thank God for loving you long before you loved him. Once you've memorized 1 John 4:9-10, make a card for someone who's lonely or going through a hard time. (Ask a parent or guardian if you need ideas.) Write these verses on one side of the card, and write your own message on the other side.

Look! I stand at the door and knock. If you hear my voice and open the door, I will come in, and we will share a meal together as friends.

Revelation 3:20

They were singing the song of Moses, the servant of God, and the song of the Lamb:

"Great and marvelous are your works,
O Lord God, the Almighty.
Just and true are your ways,
O King of the nations."

Revelation 15:3

I pray that God, the source of hope, will fill you completely with joy and peace because you trust in him. Then you will overflow with confident hope through the power of the Holy Spirit.

Romans 15:13

Be kind to each other, tenderhearted, forgiving one another, just as God through Christ has forgiven you.

Ephesians 4:32

Use your imagination and draw a picture of this marvelous event in heaven. Include the words of the victorious people's song in your picture. Memorize it by singing it out loud. We don't know what the song sounds like, so you can make up your own tune.

Glue Popsicle sticks to a piece of paper in the shape of a house to remind you of this verse. Imagine Jesus saying the words of the verse to you. Do you want to be friends with him? Will you invite him into your house—into your life—and ask him to transform it from the inside out?

Always be full of joy in the
Lord. I say it again—rejoice!

Philippians 4:4

Don't worry about anything;
instead, pray about
everything. Tell God what
you need, and thank him
for all he has done.

Philippians 4:6

God has said,

"I will never fail you.
I will never abandon you."

Hebrews 13:5

If you need wisdom, ask
our generous God, and he
will give it to you. He will
not rebuke you for asking.

James 1:5

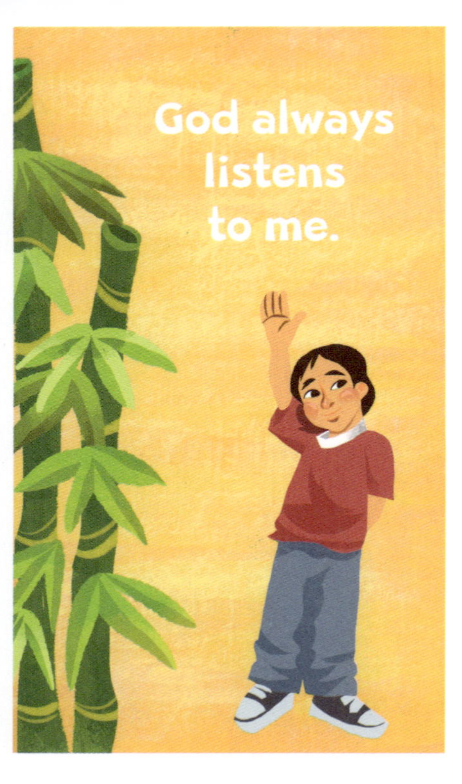

God always listens to me.

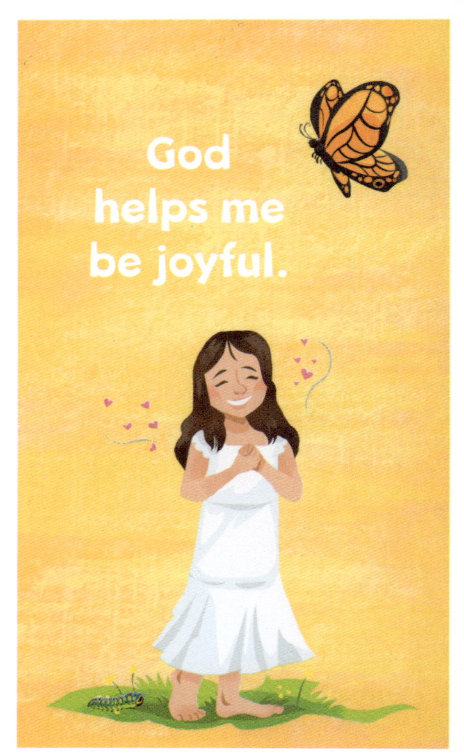

God helps me be joyful.

God hears your prayers.

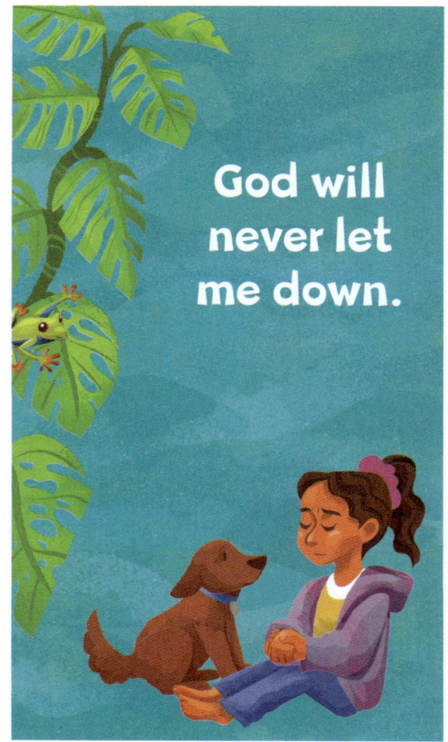

God will never let me down.